MY AFRICAN WOMAN

Adeleke Eniola Oyenusi

Published by New Generation Publishing in 2024

Copyright © Adeleke 2024

First Edition

The author asserts the moral right under the Copyright, Designs and Patents Act 1988 to be identified as the author of this work.

All Rights reserved. No part of this publication may be reproduced, stored in a retrieval system or transmitted, in any form or by any means without the prior consent of the author, nor be otherwise circulated in any form of binding or cover other than that which it is published and without a similar condition being imposed on the subsequent purchaser.

ISBN: 978-1-83563-355-7

www.newgeneration-publishing.com

New Generation Publishing

This is a work of fiction and expertise. Names, characters, places, and incidents are either the product of the author's imagination or are used fictitiously, and any resemblance to any actual person, living or dead, events, or locales is entirely coincidental.

TABLE OF CONTENTS

DEDICATION v

ACKNOWLEDGEMENTS vi

INTRODUCTION xi

CHAPTER 1 1

  My Hometown... 1

CHAPTER 2 23

  My Family 23

CHAPTER 3 35

  Arrival of Father Morgan 35

CHAPTER 4 43

  First Day of School... 43

CHAPTER 5 54

  Engagement to Comfort 54

CHAPTER 6 73

  Father Morgan Returns to England 73

CHAPTER 7 84

  Journey to England 84

CHAPTER 8 101

  Studying in England 101

CHAPTER 9 109

  Relationship with Mary 109

CHAPTER 10	124
Comfort Arrives in England	124
CHAPTER 11	132
Comfort Becomes a Nurse	132
CHAPTER 12	147
Problems with Comfort	147
CHAPTER 13	158
Moving Out of the Family House	158
CHAPTER 14	168
Graduation Day	168
CHAPTER 15	175
Comfort Took Il	175
CHAPTER 16	185
Comfort Admitted to the Hospital	185
CHAPTER 17	194
The Return to Nigeria	194
CHAPTER 18	205
The Death of My African Woman	205
ABOUT AUTHOR	212

DEDICATION

I would like to dedicate this book to all renal (kidney) patients and individuals battling life-threatening illnesses. I empathize with your struggle to survive amidst this sickness. Your unwavering determination will ultimately prevail—never lose hope.

ACKNOWLEDGEMENTS

I give glory to God, who enabled me to recover after enduring a severe, life-threatening stroke, kidney failure, and heart bypass. I found the strength to unlock my untapped potential and put pen to paper after a grueling battle with illness.

I want to express my deepest gratitude to my kidney donor and their family for their selfless decision to grant me a chance at continued life.

I also extend my heartfelt appreciation to our British government for their relentless effort in taking care of me, particularly the NHS and Social Services (Department for Work and Pensions and Housing Department), without whom my life would have been difficult.

I am sincerely grateful to my late father, Chief (Prince) Albert Olanrewaju Oyenusi, and my mother, Florence Omowunmi Oyenusi, for their pivotal roles in my upbringing.

Gisele and my three children, Princess Kimberlyne Charles, Kelvin, and Kenneth Oyenusi were a tremendous source of support and assistance during my battle with illness. I also want to thank my granddaughter, Kimaya Oyenusi, who always puts a smile on my face.

I extend my thanks to Dr. & Mrs. Johnson Ogunlowo for their support during my health crisis. You have always inspired me.

I want to extend my profound gratitude to the following individuals, listed in no order: Barrister and Mrs. Eukay

Ukandu, Professor Richard Omotoye, Dapo Sonaike, Olusina Alaka, Ayo Hundeyin, Rasak Abiwon, Johnson Owoyemi, Lawon Opesanwo, Dr. Leke Oyende, Rafiu Ibrahim, Mama B Adejumo, Aderemi Oshindeinde, Wale Coker and Niyi Odewale, your unwavering support has meant the world to me. I am deeply grateful.

The descendants of Oba (King), JS Oyenusi, led by Prince Deji Oyenusi and Princess Folahan Oyebowale, Sir (Prince) Akinola Oyenusi, Prince Adesoji Oyenusi, Princess Iyabo Sokunbi, Princess Christiana Sosanya, Princess Fela Adefule, Princess Seyi Oshikomaya, Prince Tokunbo Oyenusi, Prince Soji Oyenusi, Princess Adeyinka Giwa, Princess Adeola Fajolu, Prince Debo Oyenusi, Prince Tunde Oyenusi, Prince Tosin Oyenusi, Prince Tolu Oyenusi, Princess Kemi Oderinde, Prince Femi Oyejobi, Prince Bolaji Oyejobi, Princess Busola Olowo, Princess Adefolaju Ikutiminu, Princess Funke Obisesan, Princess Bola Oyinloye, your support has been instrumental to my well-being.

Adeleke Akinsanya, Paul Ebo, Dr. Ebenezer Solarin, Chief Yetunde Liyele, Mrs. Lola Shitabay, thank you for your invaluable support.

Chief Tunji and Mrs. Kikelomo Oyelana, my uncle and aunty, thank you for your prayers, which have been a source of strength for me.

I am inspired by our former President, Chief Aremu Olusegun Obasanjo for his meritorious service to the nation. I am thankful to Prince Dapo Abiodun, Otunba Gbenga Daniel, Senator Ibikunle Amosun, Chief Osoba for their service to my state Ogun state. Asiwaju Onafowokan, Chief Tunji Oyefuga, Aremo Awodipe, Sir Kensington Adebutu and Chief Ladi Adebutu for their contributions in Ogun state

My profound gratitude goes to our Kabiyesi, the Onirolu of Irolu Kingdom, HRH Oba Sikiru Adeyiga, my esteemed royal father. Your prayers have been a guiding light.

The Akarigbo of Remo Kingdom HRH Oba Adewale Ajayi; Elepe of Epe HRH Oba Adewale Osiberu; Ewusi of Makun HRH Oba Timothy Oyesola Akinsanya, Alakenne of Ikenne, HRH Oba Adeyinka Onakade; Alaye of Ode Remo HRH Oba (Dr) Suv. Adetunji Amidu Osho; Odemo of Ishara HRH Oba Albert Abosede Mayungbe; Olofin of Ilishan HRH Oba M Sonuga; Onipara of Ipara HRH Oba Adeniyi Taiwo; Alaperu of Iperu HRH Oba Adeleke Idowu Basibo; Ologere of Ogere HRH Oba Oladele Ogunbase; Oba of Ijebu Ijesa HRH Oba Adekoya; Alara of Ilara Remo HRH Oba Abiodun Adefehinti; Alakaka of Akaka HRH Oba J Bamidele Awoderu, my Remo Royal fathers, thank you all.

Princess Adenike Oroge, Princess Omobolanle Arojo, Princess Olaide Ladipo and Prince Adesegun, Prince Babatunde, and Prince Adeyemi Oyenusi, Biodun, Kola Adedeji, Toyin Olaitan. I sincerely appreciate your support, which has made a significant difference in my recovery journey.

Special appreciation goes to my younger brother, Prince Adeniyi Albert Oyenusi. You saw me at my lowest and highest. I always see the pain in your eyes when you visit me on my subsequent admissions in the hospitals thinking, "Is this the way I will lose my brother?" It was such an agonizing moment. But I am happy that we are still together.

My heartfelt gratitude goes to my son, Kenneth, for his invaluable advice on my writing. I want to express my appreciation to my editor, Joti Bryant, whose guidance, and support were invaluable throughout the book.

I want to thank Mrs. Boluwatife Segun-Oluwayomi, the eagle-eyed book surgeon, who did the final editing and proofreading of the book. Thanks a lot for the great job done. I am greatly impressed by your work.

My thanks also go to Pastor Sunday Adelaja of Christ Church Embassy, Dr Rilwan Bamgbala, Rev. Richard Akinboyewa, Dr. Sanni Idowu, Adeola Alayo, Bose Ali Balogun, Deacon Gbolahan Adekoya, Adewole Arogundade, Mr. Folarin Bishi, Oloye Kogbodo Oyefuga, Tope Otesanya, Femi Otesanya, Akin Otesanya, John Adebayo, Bukky Ogunlana, Ebrima Saho, Mrs. Dupe Osanyinjobi.

My profound gratitude to my fellow friends from Sayuznikis UK, Nigeria and America - Russian trained graduates.

My classmates at Remo Secondary School A level 78/80 set Sagamu, Ogun State Nigeria under the leadership of Professor Ebun Oduwole, my classmates at the Methodist Secondary Commercial College 73/77 set Sagamu, Ogun State, Nigeria, NIDO Europe and America, CANUK UK, I'm immensely grateful for your support.

Lastly, I want to thank the Irolu Development Council, Irolu Development Association, Iroluans Next Level, Proudly Omo Irolu – Social/Free zone, REMOGDF UK/IRE, Irolu Progressive Elites, Irolu Progressive Youth Association, Irolu Progressive Moment, Irolu Ladies Club, Agaunun

Prestige, Lions club, Irolu Progressive Brothers, Irolu Golden Brothers, Sekuote Sisters, members of Isese-lagba, members of the Irolu Anglican community, members of Irolu Methodist community, members of the Redeemed Christian community Irolu, members of Irolu CAC, members of Agbo Mimo Irolu, members of the Muslim community of Irolu, members of traditional worshippers, Club 7 and 8. I'm extremely grateful.

All glory to God.

INTRODUCTION

This is the story of Egunbiyi, an African young man born into a family of traditional believers in the "Ifa Oracle," in Irolu Remo, Ogun State, Nigeria.

Although his town was not large, it was a cradle of cultures. He enjoyed the varied cultural festivals while growing up.

His parents, who had struggled for years to conceive, consulted their deity and made a solemn oath that if they were blessed with a son, he would continue the family tradition of worshipping the traditional belief.

Finally, a son was born, and there was a jubilant celebration! Egunbiyi grew up immersed in the family's daily rituals of incantations, chants, and sacrifices, becoming a devout follower of the idol.

Father Paul Morgan, a white English missionary sent from the United Kingdom to lead the local Anglican Church in Irolu, played a significant role in Egunbiyi's life. He encouraged Egunbiyi to seize the opportunity for a Western education.

Father Morgan's influence was transformative, leading Egunbiyi's parents to eventually agree to his pursuit of a Western education. Initially adhering to local customs and traditions, Egunbiyi married a Nigerian girl but later had a daughter with a white woman.

The departure of Father Morgan to England left the entire community in tears as he bid farewell to the town for good.

Despite facing numerous challenges, Egunbiyi persevered and became a fully qualified lawyer, practising law in both the United Kingdom and Nigeria.

Upon returning to Nigeria, Egunbiyi entered politics and was elected as a member of parliament for his Remo constituency.

There is much more to Egunbiyi's story, but you'll have to turn the page and continue reading to uncover the rest.

CHAPTER 1

My Hometown

I was born in Irolu Remo town, Ogun state, Nigeria. It's a relatively small town, just over 92,000 square kilometers with a population of about 15,000.

One of the area's outstanding attributes is its bright red clay earth, which is immediately noticeable to visitors upon approaching my hometown.

When approaching from the south, first, there is another town called Ilishan Remo. As you get closer to my town and navigate the bend, there is an old metal blacksmith. The forge was our local vantage point, indicating that we had arrived in Irolu. It was our landmark, and it gave us such a joyous feeling.

To the north of my town is Ijesha Ijebu, to the east is Ilara-Remo, and to the west is Okun Owa.

Irolu is one of the cradles of culture. We, the sons, and daughters, are proud of our cultural heritage and all its richness.

Our cultural diversity makes it possible to accommodate all religious faiths, be it traditional believers, Christians, or Muslims.

Historically, the people of Remo migrated from Ile Ife, Osun state, Nigeria. But there was rivalry between two of the leaders, Oduduwa and Obatala, which resulted in a battle.

After the death of Obatala, some of his supporters left Ile-Ife. This led to the emergence of various communities within the Yoruba people.

During this period, the Akarigbo of Remo and his kinsmen migrated to Ijebu Ode. However, there was a conflict between the two kings: the Awujale of Ijebu Ode and the Akarigbo of Remo. So, the Akarigbo decided to leave Ijebu Ode.

Before he left Ijebu Ode, he consulted the Ifa Oracle and it revealed that wherever the calabash (large dish) he was carrying sank, upon placing it on a river, he would have to settle there.

When they reached Ikenne Remo, the calabash was placed on the river. It never sank, and Akarigbo of Remo and his kinsmen continued the journey. On reaching Sagamu, the calabash was placed in the river, and according to legend, the calabash sank in Sagamu, and they all settled at Ofin Sagamu.

Agaun-un, one of the Chiefs of Akarigbo of Remo, was among those who dispersed to neighbouring lands and acquired land for farming.

Agaun-un was a strong and an exceptional hunter. He chose to migrate to Irolu Remo because of the thick forest there, which made it easier for him to hunt bush animals and sell them for profit.

Agaun-un was the founding father of Irolu Remo.

When he arrived in Irolu, other settlers were already there. However, all parties agreed to stay together, living in peace and harmony. This was the origin of the name Irolu, which literally meant 'let us stay together.'

Irolu was a walled town in the olden days because Agaun-un built a wall right around the town. This prevented attacks from invaders during the inter-communal wars, such as those between Ijebu and Ibadan, and Ijebu and Egba.

Thus, he was able to secure Irolu from invasion.

However, one day, during the inter-tribal wars, the gate that led to the town was carelessly left open.

Agaun-un bravely proceeded to close the gates amid the fire of bullets. Because of this, Irolu was nicknamed 'Irolu Agaun Seku Ote,' which means 'Agaun-un closed the door against the invaders.'

Because of this, he was honoured and crowned the king of Irolu Remo.

Our local festivities are highly cherished by all, both young and old. All the town festivities are celebrated at a particular time of the year, each having their own significance.

We have the traditional religious festivals, such as Egungun (masquerade), Isemo (indoors)—Oro, Agbala—Agemo and Onire, Ebi (New Yam festival), and Obalufon (festival to honour the deity Obalufon, King of Ile Ife, credited with the invention of brass casting). The Christian festivals most celebrated are Easter, Christmas, and the New Year, while the Muslims have the Eid-ul-Fitr and Eid-ul-Adha.

Everyone in our hometown eagerly anticipates these festivities, as there are various exciting events. During the celebrations, the town is bustling with both residents and numerous visitors from big cities like Lagos and Ibadan, as well as from adjoining towns. The town is packed each month when there is something to celebrate.

The town is ruled by the King and his chosen traditional chiefs, of whom my father, Chief Fabiyi, was one.

Before significant town events and meetings, the King sends his spokesman to announce them to the townspeople. In the olden days, they assembled to receive news or information wherever they were in the town, or in the town square. The process of town announcement or broadcast is called 'ikede.'

Baba Afornorlor was the town crier who made the announcements. The whole town relied on him for vital information. Even without the aid of a microphone in those days, you could hear his powerful voice echoing across the town, no matter your location.

He made his announcements only in the evening after everybody had returned from the farms and markets, and moved around barefoot, carrying a kerosene lantern that allowed him to see in the dark.

He used a stick to beat an iron gong to get people's attention as he trekked from one street to another.

When we heard the gong, we all listened attentively.

His starting message was usually, 'Oba ni e gbo' meaning, "The King wants you to hear..." and the message to be delivered followed.

To appease the gods at town events and festivities, the King calls in the chief priest to the 'iledi' to consult the Ifa Oracle for advice on what to do when occasions deemed it necessary and to predict the future, using sixteen palm nuts gathered from a young tree that had never been used.

The "Iledi" is a place where the king and his traditional chiefs gather for important town festivities and meetings. It's also the place of worship for traditional believers where they gather every eight days. Additionally, it is used during the conferring of chieftaincy titles on deserving people of the town. This happens during the month of April every four years. Women are not permitted to enter the Iledi unless they are members initiated by the traditional chiefs.

In Irolu, we have Ifa priests, a profession of great significance throughout the ages. The Ifa priest divines the future of any course in life and offers advice on how to counter the effects of any misfortune.

Many Irolu sons are proficient in using the Ifa Oracle, making it a sought-after destination for people from other towns seeking solutions to their problems.

A special Ifa festival is celebrated on the $20^{th\ of}$ August each year. During this festival, the Ifa priests and women are dressed in white cotton robes, wrapped up to the chest, leaving shoulders bare.

The Osugbo cult is prominent in the town, with most of its members being traditional believers. The Osugbo drum is used to announce the death of one of their members or during gatherings of the traditional chiefs in the Iledi for celebrations.

They perform the duty of wrapping the dead body, like the mummies of Egypt, when their fellow members die. This art and ritual are passed on to a few chosen members.

Women are not allowed to see the Osugbo when they pass by for an event.

Another historical place in the town is the shrine of Esu Irolu (Satan), called the Oshi Irolu. This deity is a community god. A house was built for the Oshi Irolu, with a traditional priest always there to assist in offering sacrifices to the gods. Oshi Irolu is worshipped every five market days.

Oshi is one of the angry gods in Yoruba land, believed to be dreadful and powerful. Therefore, one must not lie, cheat, or misbehave in his presence. He is known for keeping human excesses in check, and people are wary not to incur his wrath, fearing the consequences of facing Oshi Irolu.

And all our children respect the power of Oshi Irolu (Legbara stone).

People from neighbouring towns also come to seek the help of Oshi Irolu whenever disputes arise.

Once, strange occurrences occurred in the town - sudden deaths of youths, sickness, and other inexplicable circumstances.

The king of the town sought the aid of the chief priest, who consulted the Ifa Oracle to seek answers to these unfortunate events. Ifa spoke, revealing that offerings would need to be made to Oshi Irolu to bring an end to these calamities.

The town elders and chiefs, along with the king, gathered in front of the shrine of Oshi Irolu to offer sacrifices and appease the gods. Later in the day, the sound of the Oro gong boomed throughout the town until dusk.

My father, Chief Fabiyi, held the position of head of all the masquerades in our hometown. The masqueraders were adorned in full costume, their bodies completely covered, wearing masks depicting various animals, such as the horns of a bull.

Egungun Festival - Abo Ojo is an important festival in our town, celebrated annually during the months of October, November, and December, following the rainy season.

Before the festival proper starts, at the Igbale, house of the Egungun, sacrifices were offered to the gods, followed by a feast specially prepared for the festival. Only males were allowed into the Egungun house, the Igbale.

The festival is unique. It is widely believed to be the collective spirit of our ancestors. Additionally, it is used to celebrate naming ceremonies, coronations, burials, or ritual sacrifices. It is also used to offer blessings to the spirit world and to cleanse the town of evil spirits.

During this time, my father would dress in a different attire, as the festival held great significance for him. He would dress elegantly in the traditional Aso-Oke attire, hand-woven cloth in colours red, brown, or dark blue.

He adorned himself with a red cap on top of his head and red beads around his neck, while an Itagbe draped over his right shoulder. In his hand, he held the special rod of office. This rod is a type of Aso Olona, a large wrap-around cloth from the Ijebu-Yoruba area of Nigeria, adorned with images of water spirits like crocodiles, frogs, fish heads, or snakes. The cloth is an emblem of chieftaincy, comprising a single panel approximately 1.2 meters long.

During the Egungun festival, my father wore an Alari Agbada outfit, intricately embroidered, along with sokoto (trousers) and dansiki (long-sleeved shirt), adorned with vibrant colours because of their brightness. His distinctive attire made him easily recognisable each year. Additionally, my father bought a similar set of clothes for me to wear during this celebration.

Female initiates of the Osugbo cult, known as Erelu, traditionally wear aso-oke cloth wrapped around their chests for various celebrations. The wearing of aso-oke is reserved for special occasions such as weddings, funerals, chieftaincy title conferment's, Osugbo meetings and celebrations, and is often accompanied by new shoes to mark the significance of the event.

During these festivities, my mother would also adorn herself in aso-oke attire, with her favourite being the Etu aso-oke. This ensemble typically includes a buba (blouse), gele (head tie), and iro (wrapper). Additionally, she occasionally wore adire, a form of textile art or Yoruba tie-dye, which features indigo-dyed fabrics. adire is a major local craft in Yoruba tradition.

Another one of my mother's everyday clothing choices is the popular Ankara waxed cloth. Ankara fabric is made of 100% cotton and features colourful, vibrant, tribal-like patterns and motifs. It is created using an Indonesian wax-resist dyeing technique called Batik. Originally a Dutch fabric intended for the Indonesian market, Ankara gained popularity in Nigeria due to its versatility and suitability for the hot weather, being very light.

I particularly enjoyed this period of the festival as my father had his own masquerade called Onilepaanu, meaning 'the masquerade in a corrugated iron-roofed house.' Each year, during the masquerade performances and parades through the town, all the housewives and other family members would dress in their finest attire. We would join the procession of the masquerade, accompanied by songs and the rhythmic beats of the Bata drum.

We roamed the streets of Irolu, stopping at every house along the way to sing and praise the people we visited. In return for our singing and dancing, we were graciously given money as a token of appreciation.

Throughout the festivities, all the masquerades donned beautiful costumes, adding to the vibrant atmosphere. The culmination of the festival took place on the last day at the town square, where the celebrations reached their peak.

During the festival's closing ceremony, Dad would arrive wearing a special and elegant costume, marking the grand finale. All the masqueraders would then showcase their dancing talents to the rhythm of traditional drums and songs.

The collective drumming, dancing, and feasting infused our community with glamour, joy, and a special harmony.

One of the highlights of the festival for me was the abundance of presents we received, including palm wine, yams, cocoyam, chickens, goats, and pigs. There was always an abundance of delicious food and drink throughout the festival, as the women of the town tirelessly prepared meals each day.

After returning home from the town procession, we were famished and eagerly anticipated a hearty meal. Pounded yam with bush meat wrapped in chilli pepper and green vegetables was a favourite dish. The elders and chiefs also enjoyed bitter kola, kola-nut, and palm wine as accompaniments to the meal.

Another widely celebrated festival in my hometown is the Oro festival, known as Isemo, which translates to "indoors." The Oro festival is a means of driving out evil from both the family and the town.

The Oro festival is observed annually, or during times of socio-political crises or social disruption, to restore peace and harmony among the people. It is also held to commemorate the death and burial of the king or first-class chiefs in the town.

Before the festival commences, typically in the second week of August, sacrifices are offered to appease the gods by the male chiefs, elders, and men of the town at the Igbo Oro.

During the festival, the eerie sound of Oro, resembling the barking of a dog, echoes throughout the town. The festival spans seven nights, with the main festivities occurring from Friday night until early Sunday morning, during which time the doors are closed to women.

During the main day of Isemo, which is on Saturday, men wander through the town, paying visits to friends and relatives and enjoying specially prepared delicacies. The Opepe singers also add to the festivities by singing and dancing around the town. Some of the boys who came home from Lagos were fond of singing, "Awa Lagos boys," meaning, "We are the boys from Lagos, our former capital city."

Women are forbidden from coming out during the Oro festival. It is believed that if a woman sees the Oro, she will die. The festival is unique because only men are allowed to roam the streets.

All women are in their respective houses behind closed doors awaiting visitors. Each mother or wife will prepare various sorts of food, special dishes to welcome visitors.

It is believed that the sound of Oro drives away calamities such as sudden death among the youths, epidemic diseases, and ill-luck.

The Oro festival precedes the Agemo and Onire festivals. The Agbala festival, celebrated for eight days by the Alagemo and Eluku, is a means to ensure the safety of all communities from evil spirits. It is used to cleanse the communities of any negative influences. The Onire and Agemo predominantly dance at the T-junction Road, not far from the Oshi Irolu.

The Ebi festival, on the other hand, celebrates the new yam harvest. This festival is overseen by the town king, who distributes blessed yams to the community.

During the Obalufon festival, women adorn themselves elegantly in traditional Aso Oke costumes, singing and dancing to the rhythmic beats of the Remo traditional drum called Gbedu. This annual festival takes place in the month of October. Both women and men showcase their traditional singing talents, with individuals competing to present the best songs and new melodies emerging.

The final day of the festival is celebrated at the town market center, marking the conclusion of the festivities. As the event ends, anticipation for the next year's Obalufon festival begins to build.

Participants leave the festival filled with joy and satisfaction, grateful for the opportunity to witness such a vibrant celebration.

In addition to the Obalufon festival, other cherished festivities in my hometown include Easter, Christmas, and New Year celebrations. These holidays hold particular significance for the Christians in our town, and we join in their celebrations, especially during the welcoming of a new year.

The most interesting is the New Year celebration. On New Year's Eve, at about eight o'clock in the evening, people are already gathering in all the churches in the town. Most of the Christians want to welcome the New Year in the churches. This has been a long-held tradition.

At around 11:00 pm, the New Year's Eve service commences, with the priest inviting attendees to share their wishes and resolutions for the upcoming year. People pray for guidance, protection, and blessings in the coming year.

As the clock strikes midnight, church bells ring across the town, signaling the start of the New Year. Once the Christian congregants leave the churches, we light fireworks and enjoy the vibrant bangs echoing throughout the streets. Following the fireworks display, festivities ensue in clubs and individual homes, with the youth particularly reveling in the celebrations.

Meanwhile, my great uncle, Uncle Dauda, devoutly observes the Muslim faith, adhering to all its rules and traditions, including observing religious events such as Ramadan.

During this period, Uncle Dauda and his family woke up before dawn to prepare and eat their early morning meal, after which they would fast from sunrise to sunset. Throughout the day, the town buzzed with commercial activities, with markets bustling as traders sold vegetables and foodstuff.

In the evenings, young girls roamed the town carrying trays atop their heads, selling fruits such as oranges and bananas. They carried lanterns to illuminate their path as they trekked through the streets offering their produce for sale. Many Muslims broke their fast with these fruits before partaking in other foods.

What I cherished most about this festival was visiting Uncle Dauda during this time. He and his family always prepared a variety of delicacies, ensuring there was an abundance of food to enjoy, often with leftovers.

In my hometown, the two most celebrated Muslim festivals are Eid-ul-Fitr and Eid-ul-Adha.

Eid-ul-Fitr is a Muslim holiday that marks the end of Ramadan. Uncle Dauda and his elegantly dressed family would join the procession with other Muslims, drumming and singing as they made their way to an open space reserved for the early morning prayer, a cherished tradition during this annual event. They also distribute alms to those in need. On this day, special foods and delicacies are prepared and shared with neighbours and friends.

Eid-ul-Adha, known as the Feast of Sacrifice in Islam, holds significance as it involves the sacrifice of a ram for the occasion. Three days before the festival, Uncle Dauda would travel to Sagamu Remo to purchase a large white ram for the occasion.

During this period, nearly all the Muslims in my town participate in the ritual slaughter of a white ram, commemorating the one sacrificed by Abraham in place of his son.

Before the animals are sacrificed, a special prayer is offered. The entire town is engulfed in a festive atmosphere, with celebrants dancing and strolling through the streets. It's a time of joy and abundance, with plenty of food and drink to go around.

Here is the typical noisy start to the day in my village Irolu Remo.

As early as 5:00 a.m., the first cock crows, accompanied by the continuous croaking of frogs throughout the night. Shortly after, the call to prayer from the mosque is heard throughout the town.

At 5:30 am, a church bell chimes, followed by another at 6:00 am. The cheerful melodies of various birds fill the air, signalling the start of a promising day.

In the village streets, goats and sheep can be seen trailing one another, their bleats adding to the morning chorus. Meanwhile, children reluctantly leave their homes for school, some crying and hesitant, while their mothers follow closely behind, armed with small sticks to encourage them to attend.

In Irolu, where every family knows one another, most residents are farmers who take pleasure in tilling the earth, cultivating crops, and engaging in small-scale trading.

During the Harmattan season, people in the town typically retired to bed earlier each day. The Harmattan is a cold, dry, dusty north-easterly wind blowing over West Africa between November and March, akin to the winter season.

Due to the lack of electricity in the town, as we were not connected to the national grid, households relied on traditional lanterns made from coconut shells filled with red oil on a clay plate to illuminate their homes. People enjoyed the evenings after sunset, especially when the moon was in the sky. Many families would gather outside their homes, with each family elder telling traditional folktales.

The morning routine was often initiated by the first crow of the cock at around 5:00 am, rousing the town from slumber. This familiar sound is a natural timekeeper, allowing people to gauge the hour and prepare for the day's activities.

In the early morning, farmers could be seen commuting to the fields on their bicycles, carrying hoes and other equipment in baskets made of palm leaves attached to their bikes.

In our community, mothers traditionally assumed the role of housewives. They took care of the children and managed domestic tasks such as cleaning the house, washing clothes, and cooking meals for the family.

Meanwhile, our fathers engaged in activities such as hunting for bushmeat and tilling the land. A successful day on the farm was marked by their return with bushmeat such as large rats, squirrels, snails, or snakes, as well as birds.

These catches were cleaned and then grilled or roasted in net cages over a charcoal fire. Subsequently, they would be added into a delicious tomato sauce with vegetables and plenty of chilli pepper, often served alongside pounded yam.

In my hometown of Irolu Remo, we take pride in our special dish known as Garri Ijebu, renowned for its exceptional taste and meticulous preparation. This culinary tradition has been passed down through generations.

To produce Garri Ijebu, cassava tubers are peeled, washed, and either crushed or grated to form a mash. The mash is then placed in porous bags, which are weighted down for seven days or more to expel excess water and encourage fermentation.

After fermentation, the mash is sieved and roasted in large clay pots. Many attest that Garri Ijebu boasts a superior flavour and a delightful sour tang compared to Garri from other regions.

Garri, when soaked in water and paired with sugar, roasted peanuts, and evaporated milk, offers a refreshing beverage, especially on hot sunny days, providing a cooling sensation and quenching thirst.

Eba is a dietary staple consumed daily due to its ease of digestion. It is prepared by adding Garri to boiling water and stirring with a wooden spatula until a dough-like consistency is achieved. This dough is then served with vegetable sauce or okra soup.

Ikokore, also known as water yam pottage, is a native meal of the Ijebu people. This delicacy is renowned among our community.

To prepare Ikokore, begin by washing and grating water yam, then adding a pinch of salt. In a pot of boiling water, combine blended pepper, red palm oil, and ground or whole dried crayfish. Next, form small balls of the grated water yam with your hands and gently place them into the sauce.

Add a bit of water and stir the mixture thoroughly. Allow it to cook for approximately 15 minutes until the Ikokore reaches a desired consistency. This dish is reserved for significant celebrations and festivities, showcasing the rich culinary heritage of the Ijebu people.

Ebiripo is another staple food for the Ijebus.

To prepare Ebiripo, begin by grating and salting cocoyam. Next, divide the grated cocoyam into portions and wrap them in local banana leaves. Place these wrapped portions in a pot containing two cups of water.

Cover the pot with spare banana leaves and allow the Ebiripo to boil until fully cooked. Steam for approximately an hour to ensure thorough cooking.

Once ready, unwrap the Ebiripo and serve it alongside Egusi sauce (made from ground melon seeds) or vegetable sauce with bush meat. Due to my fondness for Ebiripo, my mother affectionately dubbed me 'Baba Ebiripo,' signifying my appreciation for this dish.

My unique approach to enjoying Ebiripo involves using all five fingers to relish it with Efo riro or okra sauce. I prefer consuming Ebiripo piping hot, immediately after it is taken off the stove, especially during sunny afternoons. This indulgence often leaves me perspiring profusely, as if engaged in a culinary battle with the dish.

Once it enters my mouth, it simply vanishes down into my belly. Oh, it's yummy! Most of the time, I don't stop at one portion. I always ask for extra helpings.

Pounded yam stands as another easily digestible dish. As the name implies, it is yam that has been pounded. First, the yam is peeled, cut into small pieces, and boiled in a large pot. Once boiled, the yam is salted to enhance its flavour.

Next, the boiled yam is transferred into a mortar. Sitting down and securing the mortar between your legs, you pound the yam with a pestle until it becomes smooth with no visible lumps. Pounded yam is typically enjoyed with vegetable sauce or egusi soup. It is often prepared for important festivals or savoured on a daily basis for sheer enjoyment.

Amala, made from yam flour, is another staple food. To prepare, boil water and pour in the yam flour while stirring with a wooden spoon till the yam flour is cooked. Amala is typically enjoyed with okra soup or vegetable sauce.

In addition to accompaniments like Pounded Yam, Ebiripo, and Eba, my mother would prepare various sauces. Some of her favorites included Egusi (made from watermelon seeds), Efo riro (a vegetable sauce), tomato sauce, and okra or ewedu sauce.

Furthermore, my mother crafted two distinct homemade seasonings: the highly flavoured and scented ogiri, and iru.

Ogiri, which is made from either melon seeds or sesame seeds, is a fermented paste. To prepare it, the seeds (whether melon or sesame) are boiled until they become very soft. The resulting mixture is then tightly wrapped in banana leaves and left to ferment in large clay pots for approximately five days.

After fermentation, the mixture is smoked for two hours, then unwrapped and mashed into an oily paste, resulting in ogiri. This paste has a pungent smell and flavour.

For iru (locust beans), the process involves soaking it for seven days, followed by pounding it with a mortar and pestle. The mixture is then placed in a sieve, where the hulls are removed by rotating the sieve under running water. Next, the seeds are cooked and placed inside a calabash (also known as Opo squash or bottle gourd). The exterior of the calabash becomes hard when dried and serves as a container, bottle, or utensil.

The insides of the calabash are rubbed with wood ash, covered with leaves, and finally covered with a tray. The entire setup is then wrapped in a sack and left for approximately 36 hours to ferment, resulting in the production of Iru.

As previously mentioned, Egusi sauce was one of my mother's favourites to accompany any swallow foods. In a pot, she would add palm oil and fry small balls of egusi in the oil for approximately three minutes.

The following ingredients are added: meat, shaki (cow tripe), pepper sauce, fresh or dried crayfish, stockfish, and lastly, ogiri or iru. The mixture is left to boil, and when cooked, it can be served with any solid or protein foods.

Efo riro (vegetable sauce) was my mother's specialty and my father's favourite with pounded yam. The process involves frying sliced onions in palm oil in a large pot. Then, dried crayfish, prawns, shredded smoked catfish, or parboiled meat are added. Finally, the previously prepared ogiri or iru seasoning and chopped fresh spinach are added, and the mixture is left to boil for about 30 minutes.

Tomato sauce was another delicacy she prepared on numerous occasions. This is eaten with ewedu vegetable or okra sauce.

To cook, put red palm oil into a big pot with chopped tomato and ground hot chilli pepper. Add water, salt and iru or ogiri. Leave to boil and cook till ready.

To cook okra sauce—she would heat red palm oil in a pot and add diced okra to start frying, which starts the drawing process. She would add the following ingredients—dried fish, bush meat, ogiri or iru, and dried crayfish and cook for about eight minutes to avoid overcooking.

Ewedu—the consistency of this should be runny. Water is boiled and chopped ewedu leaves are added. A whisk is used to soften and mash the mixture continuously inside the pot during the cooking process. Afterwards, dried crayfish and iru or ogiri are added to taste.

Adalu is beans cooked in red palm oil with corn and dried crayfish.

It is common to have Ogi - dried corn or maize soaked in water for four days, ground and sieved to remove the shaft and left to settle. The excess water is removed and Ogi is left to boil for about five minutes. This is usually served in the morning for breakfast.

At times, for breakfast, Mum would prepare yam with beans in red palm oil. This dish is very filling. When we have it in the morning, we continue drinking water throughout the whole day, and it is evening before we feel hungry again.

Ogi is eaten with Akara (bean balls) or Moinmoin (bean cakes) depending on individual taste. Sugar or condensed milk can be added as a sweetener.

My mum's older sister (Lenpe) is known in town for her special dish of white rice with black chilli sauce.

This is just to mention a few of the Ijebu delicacies enjoyed by my family and me.

Unfortunately, the town of Irolu is not blessed with easy access to a nearby stream. The nearest is about a mile away. But most houses have a well nearby that provides drinking and washing water. People also depend on the rainy season as a source of water.

Most houses have a special drainage system on top of the roof that collects rainwater and pours down into big drums on the ground. This water is later stored in large traditional clay pots (called Isa) which are then sealed with clay and will stay fresh for a few months during the dry season.

These clay pots are normally stored under large trees which provide shade for the pots and cool the water. When opened, the water will taste like it has been stored in a refrigerator. We cannot wait to open the pots and feel the cooling effect of the water, particularly when the weather is very hot.

My hometown is a green belt zone with lots of vegetables. Most families grow their own vegetables, including tomatoes, peppers, okra, oranges, corn, avocados, and pawpaw.

A lot of the families also rear animals - goats, sheep, chickens, and pigs.

In the town, we have a mosque and two churches, Anglican, and Methodist. In addition to these, we have three primary schools for the three faiths, Anglican, Methodist, and Ansar-ud-Deen respectively.

We also have a night market called Oja Ale, where local food is sold to the town residents. The Ijebu people have been traders for many generations.

Most women traders sell kola nuts called *obi*. In the town, a bus travels to and from Lagos twice a week, which is important for the market traders who sell kola nuts. The bus leaves for Lagos every Monday morning and returns on Friday evening.

There is a popular saying: An Ijebu man who goes to study economics in a university has only gone to do research. We are known to be good managers, who effectively manage and save our resources.

Our town is renowned for its traditional music and dance, with the Obalufon and Opepe dances standing out as particularly famous.

During my youth days in my hometown, I found great joy in participating in these cultural activities. They never failed to captivate me, bringing moments of pure joy, delight, and happiness whenever there was cause for celebration.

Growing up, I made sure not to miss one of these cherished events.

CHAPTER 2

My Family

I am the only child of my father, Chief Fabiyi.

I was born into a family of traditional believers. My great grandparents and my grandparents were also traditional believers. They worshipped and gave sacrifices to the Ifa Oracle.

For years, my parents longed for a child, and they consulted the oracle numerous times in hopes of fulfilling their wish. Eventually, the oracle revealed to them that they needed to make sacrifices and offerings to the goddess Egungun to conceive successfully.

Soon after, my parents' prayers and offerings were accepted, and my mother became pregnant. After a prolonged wait for a male child, I was finally born, fulfilling their aspirations for a son.

At the time of my birth, there was no hospital in my town. Only a dispensary, established and operated by colonial administrators, was available. It primarily dealt with minor injuries, wounds, and basic health issues, as well as dispensing medication. While there was a small maternity ward, many pregnant women preferred to give birth at home.

In our community, we relied on experienced female elders known as Agbebi for childbirth assistance. These elders were well-trained in midwifery and passed down their skills to younger women. When the time for delivery approached, they were the ones called upon for assistance.

My arrival brought immense relief, joy, and overwhelming happiness to my parents. Given the circumstances surrounding my birth, particularly their long-held desire for a son, they provided me with everything I needed as I grew up. They believed that I brought immense joy into their lives.

Before I was born, my father made a promise to the Ifa Oracle, that if his wishes were granted and a child was born to them, that child would be dedicated to the Ifa Oracle to continue the lineage of traditional worshippers. I would serve in the house of the Ifa Oracle.

Newborns bring joy and celebration to the whole family and the community.

The Yoruba naming ceremony, also known as *isomo l'oruko,* tells the circumstances under which a child was born.

The festivities surrounding my birth lasted for a good seven days before the official naming ceremony held on the seventh day, as per tradition.

On this special day, my mother recounted that there was a gathering of numerous people, particularly from our hometown, who had come to celebrate with my parents. They expressed immense joy and excitement as my birth came after a prolonged wait for a child. The atmosphere was filled with jubilation, and the celebration was grand.

Throughout the week leading up to the naming ceremony, goats were slaughtered daily for seven days.

On the seventh day, early in the morning, our entire family, along with members of our community, gathered at our family home to partake in the naming ceremony. My grandfather, Chief Sofunke, presided over the ceremony, imparting his blessings and bestowing upon me my official name.

My mother handed me to my grandfather who held me throughout the naming ceremony. His words were,

"We thank our ancestors for this addition to the family. We seek our ancestors' blessings on his name, so that the name given will enhance his future."

He continued to explain the reason for the gathering and celebration. Then my grandfather concluded the ceremony, and I was named Egunbiyi, meaning the masquerade gave birth to him.

Each passing year, my parents continued to offer sacrifices and offerings to appease the gods, asking them to continue to spare my life and prepare me to serve the Ifa Oracle.

My father was of short stature, with a sturdy build, a dark complexion, and piercing black eyes like an eagle. His pointed nose complemented his appearance, and three distinct tribal marks on each of his cheeks, a clear indication of his Ijebu heritage.

One notable feature about my father was his lack of front teeth, a consequence of a past altercation over land disputes, according to stories from the town. It was said that during a confrontation, an adversary, unable to accept defeat, resorted to violence, striking my father with a bottle, and shattering his front teeth and jaw. The incident left him gravely injured, and only through the intercession of his father, Chief Sofunke, and sacrifices made to the gods, was his life spared.

Dad had massive and robust hands, capable of tilling multiple ridges of soil simultaneously with the traditional hoe. His remarkable strength earned him the nickname, "the powerful one with the iron hands." He was as stout as a horse.

One constant companion of Dad's was his snuff tin, always filled with *tabah*, a type of tobacco. He took great pleasure in smoking his pipe.

He bought his home-made *tabah* from our neighbour, Mama Tutu, well known in the town, being the only person who specialised in growing and grinding fresh tobacco leaves.

Each day, Dad performed the same ritual. Holding the tin of *tabah* in his hand, he tapped it against his knee to stir it, tapped it twice in the center, and twisted the tin counterclockwise to open it. He then took a pinch of tobacco in his left palm and gently squeezed it with his right hand. Afterward, he lifted a pinch and delicately rubbed it into his left nostril, followed by the right. Inhaling deeply, he waited for a moment before exhaling through his nose. His eyes immediately reddened like fire, and tears welled up. Satisfied, he would remark, "Good one." Following this, he indulged in his pipe, emitting thick, black smoke from both his nose and mouth simultaneously.

For as long as I can recall, Dad always had a red cap perched on his head, red beads on his wrist and around his neck, and his chieftain title cloth, called Itagbe, on his right shoulder.

Dad was my hero, showering me with immense love as I was the 'apple of his eye.' He often reiterated, "You are my special baby," a sentiment that resonated deeply with me, especially considering I was born in his later years.

His devotion to his family knew no bounds. I cherished him dearly as my father, appreciating his kindness and the consistently warm and cordial relationship we shared.

Dad instilled in me values of hard work and resilience, constantly encouraging me to persevere. "You must always keep trying, as long as you are alive. Be resilient, and one day your struggles will transform into happiness," were words of wisdom he frequently imparted to me.

I developed a good rapport with him and would listen with rapt attention when he recounted the trials and tribulations he faced on the path to manhood.

After indulging in his beloved palm wine during outings with his friends, Dad would become emotional and offer heartfelt prayers for my future:

"You will be an achiever in life. You will be bigger than me; you will be a blessing to your generation. You will not suffer ill-health, and you will be blessed with lots of children and grandchildren. You will not lack happiness and good health, and you will be prosperous. The gods of our forefathers will never forsake you." At the end I say a resounding Amen to his prayers.

Dad remained faithful to my mother, who was unable to conceive for many years. My mother, Omowunmi, was a gentle soul with a warm smile that lit up her face. Of average height and light complexion, she exuded a down-to-earth charm. While she was generally easygoing, she also wielded a firm hand when necessary. Yet, her greatest talent lay in the kitchen, where she effortlessly whipped up delicious meals that filled our home with warmth and comfort.

My mother was the only wife of my father. People said she was lucky to be the only one, as all my father's friends, who were also traditional chiefs, had two, three, or more wives.

It was rumoured that she had enchanted my father with black magic, known as 'black juju,' to secure her position. Given the acceptance of polygamy within our customs and traditions, many found it difficult to fathom how my mother had achieved such a feat.

"Either she has stolen your heart or brewed love potions for you," his friends would often joke, seeking to tease or provoke him. However, despite the delay in conception attributed to my mother, Omowunmi, my father never entertained the idea of taking another wife.

Omowunmi embraced the role of a full-time housewife with dedication. She diligently managed all household tasks, from cooking and cleaning to laundry and other domestic responsibilities. Such responsibilities were customary for housewives in our town and the majority of African mothers.

My father, as a traditional chief, headed all the festivals in the town. During the Egungun festival (masquerade), he was fond of doing his chants and displaying his traditional singing skills.

He was not literate, but a farmer greatly loved in the town amongst his people.

My father learnt the practice of worshipping the Ifa Oracle from his father. This skill was passed from one generation to the next at a very early age.

Daily training and teaching of the worship practices and incantations are crucial to preserving the Ifa culture and way of life.

Along with being a farmer, my father also tapped and sold palm wine, which a lot of the town elders greatly enjoyed drinking in the evening, especially after a hard day's work on the farm.

Renowned for its sweetness and great taste, my father's palm wine was considered the finest in the town, attracting a steady stream of daily patrons.

In front of the house, he built himself a special little open-air room, underneath palm trees. This place served as a meeting point for a lot of our town elders. This is where the traditional game of Ayo was played. Sharing news, information, or keeping abreast of local gossip in the town was easily done while playing Ayo and having a good time.

This was a highly popular pastime in the town, serving as a means to unwind after a hard day's work on the farm or hunting.

The Ayo game is played on a carved wooden board with two rows of six holes, and forty-eight Ayo seeds. The players sit opposite each other on wooden benches in Dad's outdoor shed with the trees providing cover from the sun and heat. The game board is called Ayo Olopon.

Ayo game requires deep thought, skill, and strategy. The players move the green seeds (omo ayo) from one hole to the other. The goal of each player is to capture as many seeds as they can by the end of the game. The player who wins is called Ota, and the loser is called Ope.

My Dad is a local champion of the game, inheriting his skill from his father, Chief Sofunke. He is a celebrity in the town when it comes to playing Ayo.

Most of the town elders would drink palm wine in the evening, and for dinner often had bush meat, roasted, grilled, or barbequed with hot chilli peppers, which was my mother's favourite way of cooking bushmeat. She also made chilli pepper soup with assorted bush meat.

Some men would purchase kolanut, bitter kola, and cigarettes to accompany their palm wine. They relished this leisurely pastime, often indulging to the point of intoxication. "Bring more." "Serve me more!" They would keep demanding for it.

Some of them would also have a tin of grinded tobacco, which they enjoyed inhaling.

Another cherished activity I shared with my dad during full moon nights was listening to his captivating storytelling. Dad had a knack for weaving various tales, and I eagerly anticipated these moments spent by the firelight in his company.

I particularly admired Dad's sense of humour, and the story of the tortoise and the rabbit remains vivid in my memory.

The story goes this way: The tortoise is always regarded as the wise one. A competition was set to take place between the tortoise and the rabbit, as each claimed to be the fastest runner.

The rabbit was a fast runner compared to the tortoise. The rabbit stated that, on any given day, he will always beat the tortoise in a race. The tortoise disagreed and said he would be the one to win the race.

So, they arranged a day for the big race. The tortoise summoned all his children and explained the situation to them. Because the tortoise knew he was no competition for the rabbit, he stationed his four children into four areas, putting them fifty metres from each other.

The race began. The rabbit, upon reaching the first fifty metres, was greatly surprised to see the tortoise in front. So, he ran faster, and on reaching the second fifty metres, he found another tortoise. He decided to run even faster. Upon reaching the third fifty metres, he met another tortoise and became baffled. He continued running to the last fifty metres, convinced he had won the race. Unfortunately, on the last lap, he met another tortoise. Eventually, the tortoise was declared the winner of the race.

The story according to my father is about being humble; do not underestimate anybody, and do not be arrogant in life.

My father also combined farming with being an herbalist, performing traditional healing. He learnt the art of mixing herbs and how to use them for healing, which was also passed on to him by his father.

At five, I was considered ready to start acquiring the knowledge of serving the Ifa Oracle. From a tender age, I started to learn and grow under the influence of the Ifa Oracle.

At twenty, I was already conversant with, and mastered the art of Oracle worship, including all the incantations which need to be memorised, the sacrifices and ways of appeasing the gods of the Ifa Oracle.

Mum also reared some farm animals - chickens, goats, pigs, and guinea fowl. She would rise very early in the morning to feed all the animals. One morning, when she woke up, she woke me up, too…

"Biyi, Biyi, Biyi!" She called out on top of her voice, as I obviously intended to continue sleeping soundly.

"Yes, Mama!"

"Get up," she ordered. "Go and bring me the bowl where I kept the animal feed, the corn."

I came out with the bowl and handed it to her.

"Biyi, do you know you will be starting the early morning incantation tomorrow?" My father asked as he stepped out of his room.

I thought to myself, *So, the day has finally arrived. I will be starting the life of an Ifa Oracle priest. I was delighted to have received the calling.* I said to myself, *this is it. I will have to toe the family line of Ifa Oracle worshippers.* I felt proud of myself.

"Alright then," I responded with excitement.

This was in the month of December, during Harmattan. The mornings were cold, and I would wrap myself in a thick blanket. During this time, I struggled to wake up, always craving more sleep.

The following morning, the cock crowed, and I roused immediately, waiting anxiously for what would happen next. I walked into the spare room where Dad kept his charms, which was also the room for worshipping the Ifa Oracle.

My father narrated the history surrounding our family and Ifa Oracle to me. He recalled how difficult it was for my grandfather to have him also, and how the Oracle came to the rescue.

My father was encouraging. He would wake me up early in the morning around 6:00am to start learning and reciting each incantation.

"Biyi, repeat after me," he would say.

"Ifa Olokun asoro mi dayo." (The Ifa Oracle turns adversary into joy.)

He would make me repeat all the incantations after him several times until he was satisfied that I had completely mastered and memorised them word for word without missing any.

The belief is that if any words are missing from a chant, it will be difficult to make things work properly. The first day went well, though nerve-wracking.

I spent the next three years learning the art of worshipping the Ifa Oracle, while other children in my town started attending classes at the primary school.

In my town, we have three faith-based schools - Anglican, Methodist, and the Ansar-u-deen, depending on which religion you belong to. The Anglican and the Methodist were established by the white missionaries to help in educating young children.

To many children, it was not only interesting but exciting to be in primary school. Olu, my best mate, also started school.

I envied him a lot. Sometimes, when he arrived home from school, he would tease and taunt me in English, knowing I could only speak my traditional Ijebu language.

Because my father explained the circumstance of my birth to me and the oath, he swore that I would worship the Ifa and forego school, I found it difficult to go against his wishes. It was painful to see some of my friends being educated in regular schools, while I was deprived.

CHAPTER 3

Arrival of Father Morgan

One afternoon, Olu came rushing to my house, beaming with excitement and eager to share something with me.

"Biyi, Biyi, have you heard the news? A white man has arrived to head the Anglican Church."

"No, I haven't."

"The news is spreading round the town like wildfire."

In most of the churches, there were priests who took charge of the daily activities and Sunday services. In the Anglican Church, it was the first time a white man was transferred to head the Irolu branch.

Though we learnt there are whites living in England, the Queen's land, we had never seen one.

"The youths are gathering at the town square," Olu continued. "Let's go and see what is happening and confirm the news."

"Allow me to put on my shirt first," I replied, as I was shirtless because it was a hot day. After getting dressed, Olu and I went to the town centre.

This was an unexpected arrival in the town. Some teenagers spotted the white Father arriving in a taxi with his luggage at the priest's residence.

Within a short time, many of the local young people nearby had gathered. We picked up courage and strolled to the gate of the rectory to confirm the story and have a proper look at him.

He noticed us approaching the gate of the rectory.

The local teens were singing and chanting:

"Oyinbo pepper, if you eat pepper, you go yellow more and more," meaning, *White man looks yellow like a ripe pepper, and if he eats more peppers, he will turn even more yellow*. He was approaching his residence as the singing and chanting continued.

As he stepped into his house, I wondered why he was so white compared to our black complexion. He looked like a ghost to me as I had never seen a white man before. He had straight, grey hair; his nose was pointed and long, and he was wearing a long white gown - like a man from another planet, taller than the average man.

He turned and beckoned to us. "Come on in. I am Father Morgan, the new Anglican priest."

But he spoke in English, and we did not understand him and were terrified of moving close to him.

We remained rooted in one spot and stared at him.

He waved his hand at us, encouraging us to come. Only Olu was brave enough to march forward while the other children pushed one another behind him.

To those of us who didn't understand the English language, his fast speech, manner of intonation, pronunciation, and expression were too much for us to handle.

Fortunately, Olu, who was already in primary school and learning English, could understand some of the things Father Morgan was saying. So, he acted as the interpreter.

Though, the Father had to repeat his words and speak slowly before Olu could fully understand his words.

"I will be of help to you whenever the need arises," he said.

I stood there, absolutely clueless about all he said.

At that instant, I made up my mind to go and learn the English language. It was a turning point for me.

Father Morgan observed I had no reaction to anything he said. He tried to speak to me slowly, but I felt shy as I still could not understand him.

He was curious about my silence and indifferent facial expression to all he had been saying and asked Olu, "Why is it that your friend does not say anything?"

Olu, ready to help me, explained my plight to him. "Because he doesn't understand nor speak the English language," he informed Father Morgan.

Father Morgan asked again, "Why is he not in school?"

"He is learning traditional medicine from his father, instead," Olu answered.

The Father then looked at me with pity and sadness, but still could not understand why I was not allowed the opportunity of going to school like my friends.

From that day forward, Father Morgan took a special interest in me, even though I was unable to communicate with him in English.

I made an effort to communicate with him in my native Ijebu language and quickly realised it's futile as he could not understand me either!

I returned home feeling so special after noticing Father Morgan's interest in me. When I arrived, I was excited and eager to break the news to my parents.

I told them, "I just came from the rectory of the new Anglican priest. We now have a white man who will be heading the church. The village youths have just dispersed from his residence. He took a special interest in me as I was among those unable to communicate with him in the English language," I explained.

I told them about my experience with Father Morgan and all that transpired in his house. But my father was unhappy and unimpressed with my story.

I sensed the anger brewing inside him, and it was as though he would explode. The thought that I was trying to incur the wrath of the gods who gave him a child at last terrified him.

Dad gave me a disdainful look, and I felt like I had been hit.

"This is it!"

"A lot has been invested in preparing you to continue the lineage of the family as traditional believers and worshippers. When you were born, we pledged you to the gods. Going against the gods' wishes will not only be dangerous but will be bound to have a calamitous ending!" My father exploded.

"You must stop any further contact with that evil one. Let this be the last time I ever hear you mention the name of that man in my house. Our forefathers have always worshipped the Ifa Oracle, and I will not stand by and watch anyone distract you from all that we represent.

"We simply cannot allow this white man to influence our way of life, and what we believe and cherish," he went on.

My mum remained numb; she had never seen dad explode in that manner.

In our culture, when the father of the house is speaking, the mother does not interfere or make comments, most especially in the children's presence. Any corrections or response to what the father says will have to be made in the children's absence. It's "Do as I say."

I stood there, shattered, and rendered speechless. I had anticipated that sharing my story would bring happiness to my dad, but it had the opposite effect. Instead of receiving praise for my bravery, I found myself chastised and filled with regret for ever opening up. His reaction left me feeling emotionally abused rather than acknowledged.

My father vehemently opposed the notion of staying in touch with Father Morgan. Following a lengthy scolding, I was forbidden from visiting Father Morgan altogether. I felt disheartened and miserable.

Nevertheless, I began secretly visiting Father Morgan without my parents' knowledge. He was consistently accessible and often had someone who interpreted for us.

Each time I visited him, he prayed with me and introduced me to the teachings of the Bible.

Occasionally, upon returning from evening prayers, Father Morgan would observe my growing interest in quotations from the Holy Book. I eagerly awaited our discussions about the Bible. Additionally, Father Morgan took the initiative to learn our native language, Ijebu.

I was nine years old when I began visiting him regularly. He was insistent about me attending primary school to start my education.

One day, when I paid a visit, he asked, "How likely is it to talk to your parents about persuading them to let you attend primary school, and to explain the good things that come from being educated?"

Upon hearing this, I was terrified of facing my dad's anger, knowing it would expose my secret meetings with Father Morgan, which my parents not only disapproved of but explicitly forbade.

However, Father Morgan reassured me, saying, "Don't worry; we will handle this like adults," sensing the fear and anxiety in my expression. With his reassurance, I reluctantly agreed to let him meet my dad.

One market day, Mum went to sell the harvest from Dad's farm. After she finished, I joined her to help pack up, and we began our journey home. Along the way, we bumped into Father Morgan and his assistant. I warmly greeted them both and took the opportunity to introduce my mother.

"Father, I'd like you to meet my mother, Omowunmi. We're just returning from the market," I said.

Father Morgan was pleased to meet Mum, and it seemed like the perfect moment for him to broach the subject of meeting with her and my father to discuss my education.

"Nice to meet you. I'm Father Morgan, the new Anglican priest. If it's convenient, I'd like to arrange a meeting with your husband sometime soon to discuss your son," he proposed.

Mum quickly answered, "Biyi will get back to you about that."

Upon returning home, Mum recounted the entire encounter to Dad. Initially, he opposed the idea of meeting with Father Morgan, but Mum eventually persuaded him to consent to it.

On the day of the meeting, Father Morgan's assistant, serving as the interpreter, was also present. Dad regarded him with disdain as Father Morgan presented my case to my parents. However, they remained unconvinced about the necessity of abandoning our customs and traditions for schooling.

Afterward, Dad informed Father Morgan that he would need a few weeks to consider the matter further. After Father Morgan's departure, Dad remained vexed, concerned that embracing education might disrupt our way of life and jeopardise the promise we made to the Oracle.

A couple of weeks later, with my mother's intervention, my dad started to change his mind.

Before granting permission for me to attend school, my parents felt compelled to consult the Oracle to determine how to annul the oath they had made. The Oracle revealed that sacrifices must be made to appease the gods once more.

Following this, another meeting was scheduled with Father Morgan, during which my parents ultimately agreed to let me pursue my education. However, they imposed the condition that I continue to learn the art of worshipping the Ifa Oracle. I accepted their terms.

Father Morgan was a source of inspiration for me. He showed genuine care and encouragement, expressing a desire for my educational success and personal growth.

I also grew fond of Father Morgan, finding great joy in assisting him in various tasks. This included fetching water from the nearby stream and occasionally gathering firewood for his cooking needs.

Behind the rectory, Father Morgan initiated a small-scale poultry farm, where he kept chickens and collected their eggs daily. Additionally, he raised pigs, rabbits, goats, and guinea fowl. Alongside this, he cultivated a modest garden, growing tomatoes, cucumbers, aubergines, bananas, pawpaw, and corn.

Occasionally, Father Morgan entrusted me to go to the market to buy essential food items, as he developed trust in me.

I took on the task of shopping for Father Morgan's favourite steak. He trusted my judgment in selecting the finest meat available at the market each day and negotiating the best price, knowing my familiarity with the market from assisting Mum with her stall.

Our market, which convened every five days, attracted people from neighbouring areas who came to our town for their shopping needs. It offered a wide array of goods, ranging from fruits and vegetables to goat, pig, bush meat, and various domestic items.

CHAPTER 4

First Day of School

At ten years old, towards the end of October, I was finally enrolled in the local primary school.

Mum woke up early and called out, "Biyi, Biyi, wake up! Have you forgotten today is your enrolment day at the Anglican primary school? We mustn't be late, as we're unsure of what to expect."

I replied, "Okay, Mum."

Swiftly, I took my shower and dressed in my uniform—a green khaki outfit consisting of knickers and a short-sleeve shirt tailored by Baba Ibeji, the only tailor in town renowned for his craftsmanship. I went without shoes.

Accompanied by Mum, we arrived at the school gate promptly, being the first to arrive. Shortly after, the porter opened the gate, allowing us entry.

Feeling a mix of embarrassment, discomfort, and shame, I couldn't shake the feeling of starting primary school at the age of ten. Most children my age were already in Primary Four.

Following my enrolment, I was guided to my classroom along with the other pupils, unsurprisingly finding myself among the oldest and tallest. Our teacher, Mr. Ayo, entered the classroom and introduced himself, after which each of us took turns introducing ourselves.

All the other children stared at me, and after the introductions, my teacher appointed me as the head of the class.

My first day at school went relatively smoothly, although I felt nervous surrounded by unfamiliar faces. I would nod if someone addressed me, but for the most part, I kept to myself.

Since it was the first day of term, we were dismissed early to go home.

The next day, we gathered at 9:00 am for early morning prayers on the football pitch. Lined up according to our classes, we sang Christian hymns accompanied by the school band. Afterward, we marched back to our classrooms.

Classes commenced with the pronunciation of the English alphabet. I felt like I was from another planet as I struggled with the unfamiliar sounds, my tongue feeling heavy with each attempt.

But I knew I had to put more effort as I was older than the other pupils and any sign of unseriousness would turn me into an object of ridicule. It was challenging...

My teacher admired me because of the extra effort I put into my studies, and I was determined to succeed in my newfound way of life.

At noon, the bell rang for break, which meant time for lunch. Mum had given me pocket money for a meal. I bought a meal of bean stew and rice, which was very tasty.

After lunch, we returned to our classroom for the afternoon lessons. With food in my belly, I was much calmer. The day went by without any problems, and I got acquainted with the school curriculum.

At 2:00 pm, the closing bell rang, signifying the end of the school day. We immediately assembled again on the football pitch for the closing prayer and dispersed to our different homes.

The parents and carers of my classmates were already waiting to pick their children, but I was old enough to go home by myself.

I returned home feeling happy and content with how the entire day had gone. My parents eagerly awaited my arrival, anxious to hear about my first day at school.

Hurrying into the house, I felt a sense of urgency to share the news. Mum stood up attentively, ready to listen, while Dad sat on the wooden chair, waiting to hear my story.

Dad asked with curiosity, "Well, how did the day go?"

Before he could finish his question, I promptly replied, "The day went well; all my fears and panic attacks disappeared. There were no unfortunate incidents."

After telling my parents about my first day at school, my mother called us to the table for dinner. She had prepared my beloved pounded yam with bush meat and vegetable sauce.

After eating, I went into my room to reflect on the first day's activities and what this would mean to me. I had to get used to this new way of life. I was determined to study hard and to succeed.

This marked the beginning of something new and remarkable in my life. Although, at first, being the tallest and oldest, my fellow pupils constantly stared at me, I soon got used to this.

The second day we were introduced to the English alphabets. A B C D etc. How heavy for me to pronounce this. After a lot of trials, I began to pronounce the alphabets with heavy tongues. But I soon got used to it.

My journey into Western education began, a stark contrast from my usual way of life, which involved early morning incantations and worshipping the gods. I found myself missing these rituals, feeling a sense of emptiness due to our traditions and customs.

That weekend, I made my way to visit Father Morgan once again, accompanied by Olu, who always acted as my interpreter. With Olu beside me, I recounted my first day-at-school experience to Father Morgan.

He was pleased with my progress and remarked, "Soon you will not need an interpreter to speak to me; you will be able to communicate on your own."

Together, Olu and I assisted Father Morgan with his gardening and fetching water before bidding him farewell and heading home.

The following day, a Sunday, Father Morgan had invited me to attend the church service. We gathered at the church, where we prayed together before dispersing. As I returned home, thoughts of the upcoming school day filled my mind.

I gathered my belongings and retired to bed early, eager for the day ahead. When I awoke at 6:00 am, I felt ready to take on the day. Each morning, the second town church bell served as my alarm, signaling the start of a new day, and prompting laborers and farmers to begin their work in the fields.

This routine repeated itself from Monday to Friday. With time, I became smarter in my studies, particularly excelling in arithmetic. My teacher took notice of my determination, despite starting school later than my peers, and he took a special interest in my progress.

He was an inspiring figure, consistently encouraging me to persevere and never give up. As the school year progressed, I found myself thriving. I completed Primary One with outstanding marks. I bagged the first position in my class and was promoted to Primary Two.

On Prize-Giving Day, I was awarded a prize for achieving the top position in my class, despite still being in Primary One. Many attendees, including parents, found this surprising. However, for those who knew me, there was a sense of interest and encouragement to witness my transition from traditional life to formal education. It was a day filled with mixed emotions for everyone present.

In Primary Two, I actively participated in various sporting events at school. I joined the school's relay team and even set a record for the fastest 100 meters ever run at the school.

As a member of the school football team, I actively participated in inter-town matches against other local schools. My teammates relied on me as I became the backbone of the team, playing in defense.

I earned the nickname 'the Iron Man at the back' because opponents found it challenging to pass me, particularly from behind. While a few may have succeeded, it often required sheer luck to dribble past me.

Amidst my dedication to football, I continued to excel in my studies. Before I knew it, I had reached the final year of primary school. It felt like just yesterday that I had begun my journey in primary education, pondering the long road ahead. And now, here I was, in Primary Six, realising how swiftly time had flown by.

I was appointed the senior prefect for the school. This was a huge responsibility for me, as I had to oversee most of the pupils during various school activities, ensure punctuality to classes, and supervise their leaving at the end of the day.

I handled this responsibility very well, never once disappointing the teachers who had entrusted me with it. It was a valuable opportunity, and they were all proud and impressed with my performance.

I was sixteen when I eventually finished primary school. Many of us had grown up, and being older than most, my classmates respected me. They knew they could rely on me for assistance and to share life experiences.

I passed my final examinations with flying colours.

On my last day at school, which coincided with Prize-Giving Day. I expected to scoop lots of prizes for being the best student and others for specific subjects. I had invited my parents for the occasion.

"Mum, Dad, please remember that tomorrow is my last day at school, and its Prize-Giving Day. I invite you to come so you can see how I've made the family proud," I reminded my parents the night before.

Dad replied, "Yes, I remember, my son."

The following day, many parents from the town attended the event, providing them with the opportunity to witness my achievements and numerous prize wins.

For some parents, it was difficult to imagine or believe that I could excel beyond the traditional practices of worshipping idols and gods. However, I surpassed my own expectations by winning more prizes than I had anticipated. The joy I felt on that day was indescribable.

Dad and mum were overjoyed and proud of me and my achievements.

After the event was over, we all returned home. Mum headed to the kitchen and once again prepared my favourite meal of pounded yam, with vegetable sauce and bush meat, much to my delight. I devoured it as if I hadn't eaten in days!

The following day, I went to see Father Morgan, who had also been at the school's Prize-Giving Day.

He took immense pride in my achievements, expressing his joy at my progress and emphasising the potential opportunities that a complete education could offer. I thanked him for being such an inspiration to me, and he encouraged me to keep pushing forward.

After our conversation, I felt even more determined to succeed in life, recognising the doors of opportunities that education could unlock for me. I was confident that I could thrive as an educated individual.

However, despite my dedication to my studies and the challenges of acquiring an education at the primary school level, my father insisted that I continue reciting and memorising the incantations and worshipping the Ifa Oracle.

Whenever I returned from school, Dad took out a special book containing all the incantations and information on herbal medicine.

This book was handwritten by the educated children of Dad's friend. He asked his friend to have his children help him write the book.

They called it the 'account book.' The account book is written in the Yoruba language. As if Dad knew that one day, he would have a son that would be able to read and use the account book.

This book was of great help to me once I began to read. He would bring the book and ask me to read it aloud to him. Surprisingly, Dad knows everything in it, word for word. And when I made mistakes, while reading sections of the book, he would correct me straight away.

"You will need to memorise this by heart," Dad said to me one day.

He never wanted me to discard this vast knowledge, the very thought of this was treacherous to him. It was the accumulated labour and knowledge of generations.

On Saturday, when I was not at school, this was the most tedious day for me, as I would have to catch up with all the incantations. And I was not finding it easy with my full school timetable.

I made a concerted effort not to upset Dad, who had initially been hesitant to permit me to attend primary school. He had already agreed with Father Morgan that continuing the practice of reciting incantations and worshipping the Ifa Oracle was one of the conditions for my schooling. I had to fulfil my part of the deal.

One of my favourite pastimes growing up was bush hunting with the younger boys from our town, particularly on Saturdays. Each of us belonged to our own group, consisting of five boys and our trusty hunting dogs.

On designated days, usually around 6:00 am, we would gather at my friend Mayowa's house to kick off our journey into the bush. We'd trek for hours before arriving at our hunting grounds. Luckily, Mayowa owned a bicycle and three skilled hunting dogs, which greatly aided us in chasing down animals once spotted, especially the elusive big bush rat.

Mayowa had a knack for discovering the holes where the bush rats were hiding. Upon finding a hole in the bush indicating the presence of a rat nearby, he would instruct us to search for the second or third hole, as bush rats often had escape routes. When spotted, the rats would dart away towards other holes.

After finding all the other holes, we began digging, with each of us assigned to stand by the holes we found along with the hunting dogs.

When he went after a rat in one hole, the rat would come running out of another hole, unaware that we had laid a siege and were waiting there with hunting dogs.

Once they jump out, the dogs are on their heels and give chase. Eventually, the dogs make the catch, most of the time. Once they caught the bush rat with their strong teeth, they would pick up the bush rat and smack it on the ground.

Another thing I enjoyed was hunting with a hand catapult. My friend, Dele, was an expert at making a hand catapult.

This consisted of a specially selected 'Y' shaped stick made with vulcanized inner tube rubber strips attached to the upright, which holds the projectile.

Daisi or Bamidele would hold the catapult firmly with their dominant hand, drawing it back far enough to provide sufficient power, with suitable-sized stones placed in it, and then released to kill pheasant, rabbit, dove, squirrel, or quail.

After killing the animal, they would call the dogs to quickly find the place where the bird or animal fell and retrieve it.

After the dogs successfully tracked and caught the prey, Dele would use a knife to cut the bird or animal. He would then allow the dogs to smell the blood, which he would rub on their noses. Additionally, the blood would be rubbed on the catapult to attract more animals, increasing our chances of successful hunting.

Another method of bird hunting we used in our childhood was using a bird cage made from bamboo to catch doves called *odere koko* in our language.

The cages were stocked with grain and strategically placed in open fields or on the football pitches of Anglican or Wesley primary schools. We felt immense excitement whenever an *odere koko*, a type of bird, wandered in to feed on the grain. As the bird indulged, the cage would snap shut, trapping it inside.

Those of us lying in wait nearby would erupt with joy at our successful catch. The captured bird would then be roasted or grilled with peppers, making it a delicious accompaniment to drink with Garri Ijebu.

Lastly, one of the most enjoyable activities was the canary bird (Ibaka) competition. These birds were placed in cages arranged side by side. As they sang, they competed against each other, with the one possessing the most eloquent voice or singing for the longest duration declared the winner. Bets were often placed on the birds, adding to the excitement of the competition.

CHAPTER 5

Engagement to Comfort

My father's neighbor and childhood best friend, Chief Adio, had a daughter named Comfort, who was four years younger than me. She possessed a gentle demeanor, with a kind and quiet nature. Her light complexion and beauty were reminiscent of a rose, with sparkling eyes that often lit up with a smile. I admired her greatly.

At the time, I was ten years old, and Comfort was six.

Initially, Comfort was quite shy and reserved. It was difficult to engage her in conversation, as she would often avoid eye contact and keep her gaze fixed on the ground whenever I attempted to speak with her.

We frequently accompanied each other to the stream to fetch water whenever our supply ran low at home. Over time, Comfort became less timid, and our fondness for each other grew.

As she became more talkative, we engaged in lengthy discussions on a wide range of topics, from family and social matters to local gossip.

One day, while walking to the river to fetch water with Comfort leading the way, we passed through thick bushes. Engrossed in conversation, I happened to glimpse a large snake ahead of her by sheer luck.

"Comfort, Comfort!" I screamed to draw her attention. "Look in front of you, there is a big snake!"

Immediately she heard this, she panicked and started screaming.

"Where is it?!" she cried.

She looked in front of her, glimpsed the big python and trembled at the size of it. I had never seen a snake that massive as well. We turned around and started running towards the house.

Thankfully, we hadn't ventured too far from town. We hurried back to my house and informed Dad, who was just about to leave for a town meeting. We recounted our frightening experience to him.

Dad quickly rallied friends and other townsmen. Dad jumped on his bicycle having with him his short gun and cutlass as they all went searching for the snake. All his friends also equipped themselves with large cutlasses and guns. Most of the men in the town were farmers and hunters who hunted bush animals and big snakes regularly. So, the prospect of hunting a big snake gave them a thrill. They wouldn't miss the opportunity of this big catch.

Dad and some of his friends quickly mounted their bicycles, and I led them to the place where we had spotted the big snake. Many other men from the town joined the search, accompanied by their hunting dogs.

Fortunately, it didn't take long for the dogs to pick up the scent, and they soon began barking to indicate the snake's whereabouts. The python attempted to slither away, but it was swiftly shot down. What a big catch it was for the town's men that day.

The dead snake was taken to my dad's house where all the local men who had participated in the hunt were gathered. The python was cut into pieces and shared among the participants, with me receiving the largest portion as I discovered the snake.

Comfort and I attended the same Anglican primary school in Irolu Remo.

Although we were not in the same class, Comfort and I were in the same school year since I started primary school later than most. I greatly admired her for her dedication to domestic chores.

Comfort's mother had instilled in her the skills of cooking, cleaning, and managing household tasks from a young age. She was also adept at fetching firewood for cooking, a common responsibility for girls in our culture. In African tradition, it is believed that women are responsible for the upkeep of the household, and its appearance reflects their care and diligence.

From as early as six years old, African girls are introduced to domestic duties, as it is thought that starting these responsibilities early will better prepare them for marriage and family life in the future.

By the time we reached Primary Four, Comfort and I had become inseparable. My deep affection for her led me to believe that she would eventually be my wife.

We continued to study together diligently until we completed primary school. Comfort was twelve years old when she finished, while I was sixteen.

Upon completion, we both took the entrance examination for secondary school in Sagamu Remo, which was not far from our town. Thankfully, we both passed the exam and were granted admission to a boarding school, away from home.

It was here at secondary school that our love for each other blossomed as we got to know each other better. Our classmates and teachers, observing our close bond, probably got a hint that there was something between us.

When we had terminal holidays, we both travelled back to our hometown.

Everybody in the town knew that one day, it was likely we would tie the knot.

The fact that our parents were best of friends made things easier, and they wanted it to happen. In the fourth year of secondary school, my parents began to inquire about my relationship with Comfort. They wanted to understand if she was the girl I envisioned spending the rest of my life with.

My father often asked questions like,

"Biyi! How about you and Comfort? How are you getting on?"

"She is fine. We are best of friends," I would answer.

"We noticed the closeness between you and Comfort, are you thinking of marrying her? Simply put, do you want to marry her?"

I firmly answered, "Yes."

I was thrilled to share my feelings with them. My love for Comfort was undeniable, and I was eager to seize the opportunity to formally engage her.

My parents were overjoyed by my response, as it aligned with their expectations.

"Perhaps we should discuss the possibility of engagement with her parents," Dad proposed.

I readily agreed.

Shortly after, accompanied by my parents and grandparents, I joined them on an official visit to Comfort's parents. We engaged in discussions regarding various aspects of our engagement and wedding ceremony. Despite Dad's close friendship with Chief Adio, Comfort's father, it was essential to follow formal procedures for such matters.

On arrival, we were warmly received, and my grandfather initiated the discussion, adhering to traditional communication protocols.

"Good afternoon, kinsmen," my grandfather greeted.

"Good afternoon," came the reply from Comfort's parents.

"We have noticed a rose in your compound and have come to pluck the beautiful flower," grandfather said metaphorically.

Laughter erupted among those gathered, adding a jovial atmosphere to the occasion.

According to our customs, it was clear we had come to seek the hand of their daughter in marriage.

"Which of the roses have you come to pluck?" her father asked, since Comfort had a sister.

"The most beautiful of the roses, tall and light-complexioned; the one who resembles an angel," grandfather answered.

"Comfort! Kate! Please, the two of you come out," her father called out. The two daughters stepped out, and I was told to point to the rose I came for, which I did.

"Comfort, do you know this man that has come to seek your hand in marriage?" her father asked.

"Yes, I do," she answered. Comfort was then invited to join the meeting as she was the centre of discussion. We were aware that her father would be delighted to see us married. He had previously confided in Dad, expressing his desire for someone familiar to marry his daughter. Being the only son, my parents were eager to welcome grandchildren into our family.

Introducing engaged couples in Africa is a family affair. The families of the bride and groom exchange visits and get to know one another.

The engagement list was carefully drafted, and both families agreed upon the amount of money for the dowry.

With the terms settled, the deal was sealed, and the meeting concluded on a positive note. My parents wasted no time in discussing the wedding date.

However, before proceeding, it was customary to consult the Ifa Oracle to assess the compatibility of the bride and groom, foresee any potential challenges, and ensure a prosperous marriage. Once this ritual was completed, offerings would be made to appease the gods before proceeding with the engagement ceremony.

A date was set for December, coinciding with our final year at secondary school. Comfort's parents provided my parents with a list of items required for the wedding, which had to be acquired beforehand. Additionally, I was tasked with raising the necessary funds for Comfort's dowry.

Typically, on a wedding day, the couple, their parents, and the entire family get beautifully dressed for the great occasion. However, the spotlight remains firmly on the couple, ensuring that nobody outshines their attire.

On our wedding day, for my attire, I opted for the timeless elegance of Aso Oke – Sanyan in a light brown hue adorned with cream stripes, meticulously hand-woven with special thread, epitomising the pinnacle of fabric choice.

My ensemble comprised a four-piece outfit, featuring Agbada – a flowing, long-sleeved gown enveloping the entire body from neck to ankle, characterised by its loose and roomy fit. This was complemented by Sokoto – trousers, and Fila – the traditional cap. To complete the look, I adorned Ileke Orun – neck beads around my neck.

Comfort's attire also consisted of a four-piece ensemble crafted from Aso-Oke – Sanyan in the same elegant hue. Her outfit included Buba – a long-sleeved blouse, Iro – a wrap-around sash, Gele – head tie, and Iborun or Ipele – shoulder sash. Like me, she accessorised with Ileke Orun and Ileke Owo – bracelets, all paired with matching shoes and bag, creating a harmonious and regal appearance for our special day.

All our parents also wore beautifully sewn Aso-Oke, while family and close friends wore Aso Ebi, which is the fabric chosen for the family.

On the wedding day, two individuals were chosen to officiate the ceremony as spokespersons for each family. These individuals were carefully selected for their familiarity with our Ijebu culture, as well as their ability to be humorous, witty, entertaining, and articulate with the ability to speak in Ijebu language.

In attendance were my parents, along with other family members, as well as the invited guests, all dressed in vibrant colors.

We arrived in the company of talking drum (called gangan) and various wedding songs. Upon our arrival, we were greeted with a rapturous welcome from the assembled guests. Along with us, we brought several items, each symbolising specific blessings for our union:

Palm wine – brings calmness to the body. It signifies that there will be calmness and peace in the marriage when difficulties or challenges arise.

Bitter kola (Orogbo) – as the name implies, signifies the couple will be together for the rest of their lives, even through life's bitterness and storms.

Kola nuts – being medicinal, bring health to the body. The couple will be blessed with good health.

Honey/sugar – the union will be pleasant and sweet.

Salt – a preservative, meaning the marriage will be preserved to old age and the couple will live to see their children's children.

Water – water does not have enemies. Their adversaries will be at peace with them.

Black pepper (Atare) – the couple will be blessed with lots of children, as this pepper has many small seeds inside.

Also among the items were goats, chicken, guinea fowl, palm oil, salt, yams, drinks, including schnapps, and clothes, according to the engagement list.

Discussions continued between the two families.

The wedding ceremony commenced with both families seated opposite each other.

The initial phase involved introductions from both families, allowing everyone to become acquainted with one another. This practice holds significance as it ensures that family members recognise each other and fosters unity between the two families through the marriage.

As the groom, I arrived accompanied by my friends, and we were welcomed into the reception area with the rhythmic beats of the Yoruba talking drum.

The wives from my bride's family spread their scarves on the floor. Then I put money on it - a token of appreciation for their cooking, cleaning, and preparing for that day.

I led my friends in greeting my bride's family, and we humbly prostrated ourselves before the seated elders as a sign of respect.

As tradition dictates, the first group of women entering does not include the bride. However, eventually, Comfort is led in, draped from head to toe, her face veiled. It is customary for me to pay for permission to unveil her face.

The bride's first destination is her parents, where she receives their blessings. With grace and poise, Comfort approached her parents, knelt before them, and they bestowed their prayers upon her.

"You will have a pleasant life as a married lady. You will be blessed with boys and girls. You will not labour to have children."

And both parents said, "Amen to the prayers."

Next, Comfort proceeded to the groom's family, where my parents and grandparents eagerly welcomed her with open arms. They expressed their joy in welcoming her into our family and assured her that she was now a cherished member of our household. They pledged to care for her with love and affection, promising to support her in every way possible. Comfort was then showered with their heartfelt prayers.

Following that, the engagement list was revisited, and Comfort's family confirmed that all items on the list had been provided as requested. Subsequently, I was called upon to present the dowry, symbolising the marriage money, to Comfort. This she accepted in the presence of everybody signifying that she agreed to marry me.

This sacred moment was met with a resounding applause from all family members, signifying their approval and support for our union.

Chief Adio, Comfort's father, poured palm wine into the traditional calabash cup and held it out to her.

"Stand up, and go and give it to your husband to drink," he instructed.

Escorted by her friends, Comfort approached me and gracefully knelt before me, offering the ceremonial drink.

This part of the ritual was always fun, as often, the bachelors present at the ceremony would tease the bride to come and give them the drink meant for the groom.

With a smile, Comfort presented me with the palm wine, which I gladly accepted and drank from. In return, I offered her some to drink as well.

Following this exchange, Comfort then presented me with a cap, symbolising the husband's role as the crown on the woman's head, signifying his position as the head of their family. As per tradition, Comfort knelt as I drank the palm wine. This is a mark of respect.

Afterward, we joyfully took to the dance floor with our guests, who joined us in celebration, showering us with money – which we really enjoyed!

Comfort's parents graciously treated us to a sumptuous feast, featuring a variety of special delicacies from the Ijebu culture. The menu included pounded yam served with either vegetable or egusi sauce, white rice paired with a special chilli sauce, Ikokore and Ebiripo—both Ijebu specialties—accompanied by vegetable or egusi sauce, beans with fried spicy sauce, beef, fish, chicken, fried red plantain, and steamed ground beans (Moin-moin), all meticulously prepared for the occasion.

Amidst the joyful atmosphere, we indulged heartily in the delicious spread, and there was an abundance of food for everyone to enjoy.

Following the feast, Comfort and I were officially pronounced husband and wife. According to our tradition, it was time for Comfort to be formally welcomed into our new family home. She was escorted by her friends and family members to embark on this significant journey.

Upon arriving at the husband's family home, a customary ritual took place before Comfort entered the house. This ritual involved washing the new bride's feet as a symbolic gesture to cleanse her of any negative or bad spirits that may have accompanied her.

Prepared with warm water, soap, and a towel, the groom's family, along with the gathered wives, facilitated this ritual. The most senior wife took the lead in washing Comfort's feet, imparting blessings, and offering prayers for her well-being and the harmony of the family now that Comfort was married into it.

Through this act of foot washing and the accompanying blessings and prayers, it was believed that any potential negative energies or influences were dispelled, ensuring a prosperous and harmonious beginning for Comfort in her new family home.

Later in the ceremony, Comfort was presented with a large calabash to trample on and break, a tradition symbolising the number of children she would be blessed with in her marriage. The number of pieces she broke the calabash into was believed to indicate the number of children she would bear. With this in mind, every woman makes an effort to break the calabash into as many pieces as possible. Comfort successfully broke the calabash into seven pieces, signifying the hope for a fruitful and abundant family life.

Following this symbolic ritual, my grandmother, as the maternal head of our family, took Comfort under her wing and led her to the oldest wife in the household. This esteemed woman would serve as her mentor, offering guidance and support as she adjusted to her new role within the family.

On the night of the wedding, a white cotton gown was laid out on the bed for Comfort to sleep in. This tradition symbolised her purity and virginity, reflecting the honour and integrity of the family. It was considered a disgrace to the family if the bride was discovered not to be a virgin on her wedding night.

The morning after the wedding, my family presented Comfort's parents with a large rooster as a token of appreciation for her purity. Furthermore, the wedding bedsheet, stained with blood from Comfort's hymen breaking, was carefully washed, and preserved. According to tradition, this sheet would be kept until the birth of our first child. Upon the arrival of our firstborn, the sheet would be retrieved and used to wrap the baby during the naming ceremony, signifying the continuation of our family lineage.

My parents were overjoyed to witness my marriage, a momentous occasion that fulfilled one of their deepest desires as African parents. Their hearts swelled with anticipation for the next chapter: the arrival of grandchildren, a cherished milestone in our family's journey.

But Comfort and I agreed we will only be ready to have children after finishing secondary school. We kept and stood by this promise we made to each other.

We finished secondary school, left the boarding house, and returned to our hometown.

I secured a job as a clerk at the Public Works Department in Sagamu, a nearby town, following a successful interview. Meanwhile, Comfort embarked on her career as a teacher at the Anglican primary school in our town. During this period, primary school teachers didn't require specialised training, and Comfort readily embraced her new role.

I rented a room in Sagamu, located near my place of work, and I returned home every weekend to be with Comfort.

I could not wait for Fridays to arrive; I counted the hours each week until I could jump in a taxi and travel back home to spend the weekend with my new wife.

Initially, Comfort was living with my parents where I maintained my own room. As our financial situation improved, we decided to rent an apartment in town. In this new living arrangement, Comfort shared the apartment with one of her nephews, who assisted with household chores. For us Africans, it is normal to invite one of our nephews to live with us.

I loved Comfort's passion for cooking and her dedication towards the family. The respect in the house was mutual.

Shortly after, Comfort became pregnant. When we shared the news with my parents, who had eagerly awaited this moment, they were overjoyed. They expressed their excitement and happiness, knowing they would live long enough to meet their first grandchild.

Mum often visited Comfort to assist her during the pregnancy. She and my father could not wait to see the birth of their grandchild. As the due date approached, the excitement in our household grew palpable.

One weekend, while I was seated in the lounge at home, Comfort, resting in the bedroom, called out to me, "Biyi, I'm feeling terrible. I'm experiencing both heat and cold at the same time, and I have pain in my stomach."

I immediately sent her nephew to quickly go to my parents' house and fetch my mother. Soon after, she arrived. Knowing that Comfort's delivery was imminent, my mother and I wasted no time in transporting Comfort to the nearby dispensary, where trained nurses and midwives were available.

I started to panic, not knowing what to do or say. Comfort was now in labour and screaming in pain, which sent shock waves throughout my body.

Experiencing Comfort's labour pains for the first time filled me with a profound sense of empathy and concern.

Her eyes were red, and she was mumbling strange things. I could not make out what she was saying.

I had hoped to witness my first child being born, to share in the experience and witness the baby's delivery, but I was not allowed in the delivery room. It was deemed unconventional for the husband to be present during his wife's childbirth.

Thankfully, the delivery went smoothly, and both mother and baby emerged in good health.

"You have a boy!" my mother exclaimed, announcing the joyful news to me.

"Are you sure?" I asked eagerly.

"Yes!" she affirmed.

My heart swelled with happiness and overwhelming joy, as I had eagerly anticipated the arrival of a baby boy.

After three days, my wife and son were discharged from the dispensary and returned home. I felt a wave of relief wash over me as they arrived home. It was a reality; I was now a father! Suddenly, I felt a sense of maturity settle upon me, with the weight of responsibility resting squarely on my shoulders.

On the seventh day the naming ceremony took place, graced by many from both families. My father performed the ceremony.

Early in the morning, we all gathered at my family home. My father began the ceremony by first expressing gratitude to our ancestors who had blessed us with a son in the family.

"We thank our ancestors for this new addition to our family and seek their blessings upon his name, ensuring it enhances his future," he proclaimed, pouring palm wine on the ground as a sign of respect.

He went further to explain the reason for the gathering and celebration.

"Today, we are gathered because Egunbiyi and Comfort have brought into the family a new life. And we have brought the traditional items to perform the ceremony."

"The items used in everyday life hold symbolic significance: water, salt, honey, sugar, kola nut (obi), bitter kola (orogbo), palm wine, dried catfish, palm oil, and alligator pepper (atare and aadun)," my father explained. "We call upon our ancestors to bless these items and the child."

The gathering responded, "Ase," meaning *So shall it be,* signifying agreement.

Next, my grandfather, Chief Sofunke, addressed the gathering. "Today, we offer palm wine to our ancestors as libations, inviting them to join us and bless our child."

Again, the gathering answered, "Ase."

Comfort's grandfather, Chief Ajewole, addressed the gathering next.

"We offer water, as it has no enemy. Everything in life depends on water to survive. May the child never be thirsty, and may no enemies hinder his growth."

The gathering responded, "Ase," affirming the wish.

Then it was my father, Chief Fabiyi's turn to speak once more. "The bitter kola (orogbo) lasts longer than other kolas. May this child have a long life."

The gathering responded, "Ase," in agreement.

The first man of honour, Chief Adio, Comfort's father, spoke again.

"The black pepper has many seeds within its fruit. Our grandson will bear lots of children."

The gathering answered, "Ase," in agreement. It was now my mother, Omowunmi's turn to speak.

"We use palm oil to prevent rust. It helps to soothe and massage the body. The child will have a smooth and easy life."

The gathering answered "Ase." The first woman of honour, Mama Iyabo, Comfort's mother, addressed the gathering next.

"Salt is used to add flavour to our food. The life of our grandchild will be filled with happiness and flavour."

"Ase," the gathering answered.

The second man of honour, Chief Adesegun, took the floor.

"The catfish make use of its head to find its way in the water. Our grandson will find his way in life and will wither any rough times."

"Ase," the gathering answered.

My Aunt Bimpe spoke next.

"Kolanut (obi) is chewed and then spit out. Our child will repel all evil in his life."

The gathering answered "Ase." My Uncle Dauda spoke next.

"Honey is a sweetener. The life of our new son will be sweet and happy."

The gathering answered, "Ase."

My father concluded the ceremony.

"The boy is named Ayodele, meaning *joy arrived home*."

My mother packed her belongings and came to live with Comfort to give her much-needed help during this time. She took on the task of cooking for her and bathing the newborn baby ensuring that both mother and child received proper care and attention.

Additionally, every morning, she assisted Comfort with the healing of her womb and stretch marks on her tummy. This involved warming broken clay plates over the fire to wrap around her tummy. This traditional African method is commonly used by many women for postpartum recovery. She faithfully performed this ritual for over three months.

Comfort's mother was also paying her visits. She assisted by taking care of the baby and handling some of the domestic chores. My mother and Comfort's mother alternated weekly to provide support and assistance.

My poor mother not only took care of Comfort but also had to hurry back home each day to attend to my dad. During moments when things were a bit calmer with Comfort, she would swiftly go and prepare meals for my dad. Essentially, she was managing two households simultaneously.

However, when I came home on the weekends, things improved slightly for her as she could spend more time with Dad.

Aside, the body healing she did for Comfort, I handled other tasks, particularly domestic chores, to ease Comfort's burden.

CHAPTER 6

Father Morgan Returns to England

Father Morgan served as the resident priest for the Anglican Church in my town for fifteen years. He successfully converted many traditional believers to members of his congregation through lots of activities in the church, from Easter holiday to Christmas and New Year celebrations, morning prayers, christenings, and baptisms during his tenure. He also encouraged more young children to take up education.

I had an exceptional relationship with Father Morgan. He was an inspirational spiritual father and confidant.

Even though I lived in Sagamu Remo due to my work, whenever I visited my hometown, no matter how brief, I made it a point to visit him regularly and he was always delighted to see me.

"How is your work going? Are you enjoying your new home?" he inquired every time.

"I am fine and coping fine," I would answer.

I often helped him with his domestic work: gardening and feeding the animals. His stock of animals had grown over the years. The number of chicken cages had also increased from one to five with ten chicken layers in a cage. The chickens were kept inside for laying eggs while all other animals were allowed to roam the compound.

I loved feeding the roaming animals. Watching them run to me to feed when I scattered the grain was pleasurable. He also had ten fully grown pigs living in a special shed. My mum helped in selling any excess eggs or animals in the market.

During the Easter, Christmas, and New Year festivities, I always celebrated with him which fostered a closer relationship. He counselled me on a range of life issues.

One day, I paid him a visit. He informed me about the Anglican Church scholarship offering students the opportunity to further their education in England. He said it was an excellent opportunity to further my education.

"Are you interested in applying for the scholarship?"

"Yes, yes, I am interested. Thank you very much."

Then he went over to the old beautifully crafted cupboard by his piano in the sitting room. He gently unlocked it and brought out a brown envelope that held the applications. He pulled out one of the forms and handed it to me.

"Take this application and read it thoroughly first. Then fill the form and return it to me before setting out to Sagamu."

"Thanks, Father," I said, beaming with joy.

He also reminded me of his imminent return to England and soon he would be heading back.

I joyfully left his house, praying that I would be fortunate and be accepted. On getting to my house, I told my family about it, and they were all excited for me.

On one of my subsequent visits to my hometown, I paid a visit to Father Morgan as usual. He flashed a smile as soon as he saw me, "Congratulations, Biyi."

I wondered if that meant I was successful and was awarded a scholarship, knowing that Father had earlier recommended me.

"Your application was successful. You have been chosen for the scholarship."

My heart leapt for joy. I was so excited that I couldn't find the right words. Without a second thought, I hugged Father tightly and exclaimed,

"Thank you, Father! Thank you, Lord!"

"So, the first thing you need to do now is apply for your international travel document, a passport," he informed me.

When I heard this, I was over the moon. My joy and happiness knew no bounds. My dream was about to become reality: I was going to England, the white man's land.

I hurried home to break the news to my family. I told my father that I would first need to visit Lagos to obtain my passport. Fortunately, my uncle, Dad's younger brother, worked as a taxi driver in Lagos. Therefore, Dad suggested I should go to him, and he could help me find my way around Lagos.

Dad retrieved a piece of paper from his room on which he had written down his brother's address in Lagos. He then gave it to me to copy.

Lagos was our capital city, but I had never been there. I had only heard nice stories about it having bridges and being surrounded by water. Our capital city had lots of skyscrapers, being the commercial nerve centre of the country. But this time, I must visit for my travel documents, not sightseeing. My mission in Lagos was to apply for my international passport, so I could travel with Father Morgan.

I left Sagamu early in the morning to the bus station to catch the commercial bus that plies Lagos. Uncle Bayo lived in Lagos Island and to get to him, I would need to cross the Carter Bridge, which connected Lagos mainland to Lagos Island.

It was a fascinating experience for me, being my first opportunity to get acquainted with Lagos and its environs.

I arrived at the Yaba bus station, Uncle Bayo's point of operation and where buses from Sagamu end their trip. Uncle Bayo nicknamed the 'Ijebu Man,' was popular at the bus station. I enquired about him from the bus station manager. He informed me that Uncle Bayo had just left with a passenger and should soon be back in forty minutes. I agreed to wait for his return when asked as Uncle Bayo was the person I needed to see.

After about fifty minutes, Uncle Bayo returned to the bus station to find me waiting for him. Upon seeing him, I prostrated to greet him as our tradition demanded. Eventually, he closed for the day, and we were on our way to his home. We crossed the famous Carter Bridge, and we could see some captivating sites of Lagos Island. On our arrival, his wife and family welcomed us warmly. She prepared a meal of rice and beans for us. We had a wonderful dinner after which we retired for the night.

The following day, Uncle Bayo and I went to the passport office to apply for my Nigerian passport. I filled out the application and submitted it promptly. The officer-in-charge told me to come back in ten days.

With our mission accomplished, Uncle Bayo drove me to the bus station to board a bus back to Sagamu.

A few weeks later, I returned to Lagos to collect my passport, which I brought to share with Father Morgan and my parents in town.

The news that I would be travelling to the white man's land spread like wildfire throughout the whole town. One day, one of my friends, Niyi, whom I hadn't seen for a while, happened to pass by some girls coming from the river. As they gossiped, he overheard one of them say, "It is spreading round the town that Egunbiyi got a scholarship from the Anglican Church and will be travelling to the white man's land."

On hearing this, Niyi rushed to my house to confirm the news and met me at home.

"How are you, Egunbiyi? Quite some time now. I've hardly seen you since you started working in another town. We hear you return home once in a blue moon," he said.

"Apologies, Niyi. Yes, I only manage to make it home on weekends. By the time I do one thing or another, it's already time to return" I replied.

"Is it true you are travelling to the white man's land? I overheard some ladies coming from the stream talking about it."

"Yes, it's not a rumour, it's true. I will be travelling to England to further my education. I secured a scholarship to study in London through the Anglican Church."

"Oh, congratulations. I am delighted for you. May things go well for you there. May the gods of our forefathers lead and bring you back safely."

"Amen." I answered.

"Don't forget about us, your friends, and the town. If we don't see each before you leave, then have a safe trip," he said and left.

The news delighted some people while others got envious of my celebrity status and of my dad whose only son would be going with Father Morgan to England.

But the idea of leaving my family became a major challenge. I still couldn't believe I was going to leave them and travel all the way to England. Although excited, the thought of leaving everything I cherished behind for an unknown journey was daunting.

But I kept staring at my passport, the anticipation of being in England soon to further my education filled me with immense joy.

Father Morgan had to return to London in the month of September, after his service in my town was over. I also had to resign officially from my place of work.

But I discovered I needed to give at least a month's notice before I could claim all my entitlements which made it impossible for me to travel with Father Morgan. Therefore, he would leave for England without me. I would join him over there within a few months, however.

I officially resigned from my position as a clerk at the Public Works Department in Sagamu Remo and returned to my home to stay with my family.

The Church organised a farewell party for Father Morgan. Everybody was filled with joy and spoke positively about him, highlighting the significant impact he had on the lives of the people of the town. It was a heartfelt and well-deserved send forth. Many people, both young and old, shed tears during the emotional farewell.

On the day of his departure, the entire town came to bid him goodbye. He was escorted to the town border with everyone following his taxi, and he waved his final goodbye as the taxi drove off towards Lagos.

Since I couldn't travel with Father Morgan, I was expected to make the journey alone from my town to Lagos. However, I was unfamiliar with Lagos, having only been there twice before when I went to obtain my passport.

In December, a day before my departure to England, my father gathered the chief priest of my town and some town elders together. Sacrifices were offered to Ogun, the god of Iron, seeking his mercy. Additionally, a consultation with the Ifa Oracle about my journey was conducted.

The Ifa Oracle revealed that the journey would be safe and successful. Following the consultation, ritual sacrifices were made accordingly.

There was an abundance of food, including Akara (bean balls), Ikokore, and Ebiripo, traditional Ijebu-Remo dishes. Additionally, there was vegetable Egusi soup and dried smoked fish, accompanied by the customary palm wine.

Dad went out to tap the early morning palm wine, deemed to be freshest and at its best soon after sunrise. He invited all the town elders for a feast. Masquerades, dancing, and parades filled the streets, commemorating my journey to the white man's land.

The following morning, my father chartered a bus, with the town elders and others in masquerade, to accompany us to Lagos as an entourage.

As soon as the early morning cock crowed, the town elders were already gathered in front of our house. Thirty minutes later, we departed for Lagos. It was a beautiful morning promising a sunny day ahead.

The town elders were overjoyed, as this was their first trip to Lagos. They were happy for my father, that his only son was successfully chosen from the youths in the town to journey to the white man's land for study.

For many town elders, seeing aeroplanes for the first time was a fantastic treat. They were amazed by the skyscrapers, big markets, wide roads of the city, and modern bridges. This marked my third visit to Lagos. My first visit was to my uncle who resided in Lagos Island while the second was when I returned to pick up my passport.

We eventually arrived at the Lagos International Airport. The masquerade procession commenced, accompanied by traditional songs, drumming, and dancing - all to wish me well on my travels.

My father, overjoyed and a bit overwhelmed by it all, danced with an exuberance I had never seen before. After much dancing and singing, the hour of my flight departure drew near.

The town elders started their prayers, invoking the blessings of the gods of our forefathers to lead me in all my endeavours and ensure my safe return to Nigeria. My mother appeared less emotional this time than my father who was already in tears, his eyes streamed like an open tap. He eventually gathered the courage to conclude the prayers.

Finally, it was time for me to leave. I embraced all the town elders, dad, mum, and lastly my wife and son.

Comfort and my son cried as though it was my last day on earth.

"Say bye to your dad," Comfort urged my son, Ayodele, who was now almost four years old, as she held his hand to wave me farewell. My eyes were swollen with emotion. I was in a totally confused state, but I had to go; nothing was going to stop me from travelling.

I pushed aside my emotions, hurried forward, and waved goodbye to everybody.

Mum burst into tears. I immediately returned to console her and said to her, "Mum, I am not going forever, I will soon be back. You just watch! I will soon be back."

I thought to myself, *if you don't muster up enough strength, you won't make it onto this plane!* Therefore, I summoned the courage and forged ahead, waving to everyone along the way. I proceeded through customs and immigration and prepared to wait for the boarding announcement. It was nighttime when we were finally called to start boarding.

This was my first time on an aeroplane, and I suddenly became nervous, feeling panic set in. I couldn't understand why this was happening suddenly. As I stepped onto the plane, my legs started to shake. I searched for my seat number and upon finding it, I took my seat.

I couldn't understand why I was sweating profusely. I retrieved my clean handkerchief and wiped my face, only for it to be soaked immediately. Thankfully, my seat was by the window, allowing me to look outside at the surroundings and distract myself a little before takeoff. I was on a British Airways flight from Lagos to London with a stopover in Kano, Nigeria. It was the new express once a week service, every Thursday, with a total elapsed time of eleven hours and fifty minutes. This was a significant improvement over the service previously offered by Britannia, which took three hours longer.

As the flight was about to take-off, the hostess came forward and explained the safety procedure to the passengers, then announced,

"The plane will be taking off from Lagos any moment now. We anticipate arriving on time in both Kano and London, England. Once we are near Heathrow Airport in England, we will provide you with a report of the local weather."

As the plane began to slowly move along the tarmac, the realisation that I was about to fly started to sink in. Eventually, the plane gained speed on the runway, with the engines at full throttle. With less lift than I expected, the plane took off.

I was now high above the clouds and flying!

I bid Nigeria goodbye, carrying with me prayers for success in all my undertakings in England, and hoping to return home with the Golden Fleece.

I began to count the hours and minutes until my arrival in London.

CHAPTER 7

Journey to England

On Wednesday, the night of December 15, 1962, I boarded BOAC Flight 264 departing from Lagos and arrived at Heathrow Airport in London on Thursday morning.

I was amazed that the journey had ended, and we were about to leave the aeroplane.

After waiting for the first-class passengers to get off, I was delighted to finally alight from the plane. I was amongst the few blacks on the flight. Most of the people that travelled with me were white expatriates; many of them stared at me.

As I came out of the plane, I looked to the heavens and said to myself, *this is it. I am in London.*

To my amazement, the ground outside was completely covered in white crystals. And it was freezing cold!

I descended the short metal stairs of the plane and proceeded toward the waiting bus that would transport us to the airport building, specifically to the Arrivals Hall.

I jumped inside the bus parked nearby, waiting for the remaining passengers. I was shivering; I regretted not wearing warmer clothes.

On getting off the bus, I was directed to the immigration desk as I needed no visa to enter the United Kingdom.

On approaching the Immigration services, they threw a series of questions at me and my reasons for visiting. I immediately showed them the Telegraph I received from Father Paul Morgan about my scholarship to study in England. My passport received its stamp, granting admission until 1967, after the end of my studies.

Then I went through customs, where my bags were quickly searched. After which I made my way through to the Arrivals area.

What a big contrast between my Nigeria and England. I felt overwhelmed by the many differences. The massive airport was squeaky clean and the gigantic buildings were well-structured. Father Morgan was waiting for me at the Arrivals meeting point. I had sent him a telegram giving him details of my exact flight and departure, and my time of arrival at Heathrow Airport, London. That made my journey more straightforward.

I noticed him where he stood, patiently waiting, but still could not believe it was really him. The last time we met, we were in my hometown of Irolu, and now we are in London, England. What a wonderful experience. He noticed me first, waved at me and shouted,

"Biyi, Biyi, over here!"

My eyes quickly scanned the crowd of waiting passengers, and there he was: Father Morgan, wearing a wide grin.

I returned the smile and hurried straight to him, where he enveloped me in a big hug.

"How was the journey? I hope it wasn't too boring." he asked.

"Fine sir, I enjoyed the trip. It was an astonishing experience. Unlike anything I have ever experienced. It's a pleasure to be with you again. Thanks for everything you have done for me. I do appreciate all your help. I sincerely appreciate your influence in my life. The almighty God will continue to shower his blessings upon you. Amen," I replied in one breath.

"Well, welcome to London, capital of the United Kingdom," he said.

"Thank you, sir," I replied.

The temperature outside the terminal was freezing cold, especially compared to our climate back home in Nigeria, which was hot most of the time.

Fortunately, he had brought an extra warm jacket along and he handed it to me.

"Put on the jacket, it should keep you warm. I thought you might not have one with you," he said.

I immediately put on the jacket and started warming up.

"Would you care for some breakfast?" he asked.

I was starving; it felt like the unaccustomed cold had taken the life out of me. I was hungrier than I expected.

Without hesitation, I replied, "Yes sir."

We proceeded to an airport restaurant and had a breakfast of fried eggs and toast with jam and tea or coffee. Though I was not used to this sort of meal, especially to start the day, I was famished that anything would do to revive me.

We chatted about my town and all the other people he knew in Nigeria. Surprisingly, he remembered everybody he left.

Afterwards, we shifted our attention to my new home, London.

He briefed me,

"We are now in the beginning of winter, which will last a couple of months. We had a lot of fog at the beginning of the month. Strong winds brought snow to the country on the 12th and 13th December, and the temperature plummeted. We now have a big freeze."

I was speechless and overwhelmed, faced with the reality of how I would have to live for a few months in this blood-curdling weather.

We left the airport and made our way to the car park where he left his car.

As I stepped outside, I saw the whole area was crystal white and covered with snow.

"Whoo!" I shouted. "What an experience!"

This was my first encounter with snow covering the ground, especially over such a large space. I had imagined it before and seen pictures of it in story books, but experiencing it firsthand was entirely different. I had seen flakes of ice in the freezer, but what I beheld here was beyond comparison. It was a sight unlike anything I had ever witnessed in my life.

I promptly turned to Father Morgan and asked,

"May I touch the snow and scoop some in my hand to have a feel?"

"Of course," he replied, laughing at my astonishment.

I reached out and touched the snow, feeling its brilliant coldness. Once again, I pondered if I would survive in this environment.

Father Morgan, as if he knew what was going through my mind, quickly gave me the assurance I needed.

"Oh boy, don't bother yourself with the cold weather. You will cope with it very well."

At that moment, I became convinced that life in London would be manageable.

He got into the driver's side of his small blue two-door Ford Cortina while I slid into the passenger side.

"It's called the small car with a big difference," he informed me when I inquired about his car.

It had a spacious interior, stylish, and neat. "The engine can do a top speed of seventy-seven miles per hour," he added.

I happily settled into the car, and we drove north for about two hours. On our way out of the city, I observed many well-structured, tall, and magnificent buildings.

In my town, we had no multi-storey buildings or long, wide boulevards. The unpainted houses were built with red clay and bricks, topped with roofs made from palm trees. Many of these homes had sheds where we kept the animals we raised.

During the day, young girls roamed about with trays on their heads hawking fruit, vegetables, palm oil, bread, and small items for daily use.

Nigerian towns are green, with lots of palm trees and plants. Also, the buildings are usually scattered compared to a city like London where the houses are in rows and in proxy to one another.

My town boasts of just one straight road that goes through and connects to adjacent towns, without any signs anywhere. Whereas in London, the roads are clearly marked and well-connected, with lots of helpful signs. The difference between my town and London is outstanding!

There were also coloured traffic signals, which controlled the movement of vehicles on the roads. I had never seen such a multitude of cars in my entire life. In my hometown, we only had taxis that sporadically served the town, and buses that travelled from the town to Lagos, our capital city, twice a week.

We drove on a motorway. Father told me that the motorway halved our journey, compared to driving on smaller roads, where the speed limit was lower. It was like the motorway was created for fast and furious cars.

We arrived at a residential area on the outskirts of the city, with lots of houses and pulled up in front of one. It was an attractive semi-detached house, adorned with green trim, a garden and trees in front, along with a garage. After parking the car in the garage, we entered the house.

"Welcome to my house. Feel free. It's also your house now," Father told me. Tired from the long journey and desperately needing a good sleep, I couldn't wait any longer. I was soon shown to my own room.

I eagerly climbed into the bed, which was adorned with thick blankets—a stark contrast to back home, where I didn't even need a sheet to cover myself while sleeping due to the intense heat. Here, I found myself needing to cocoon myself in a thick blanket, even while wearing night clothes.

Within minutes, I fell into a deep sleep, like a newborn baby.

I didn't stir until the following day.

"Biyi, Biyi, wake up. It's breakfast time. Wakey, wakey!!"

The mattress cradled my entire body as I slept, allowing me to sink into its embrace. I was still immersed in a pleasant dream, enjoying the thick, comfortable mattress when Father's voice roused me. The aroma of food hit me straight away.

Waking up, I felt more energised. Getting up in the morning was much easier than it used to be, compared to sleeping on a hard, dried grass mattress back home in Nigeria, where the distinct smell of the grass stuffing would linger.

I went downstairs to join Father for breakfast. On my way to the dining table, now wide awake, I had the opportunity to take a good look at the house.

The sitting room was spacious with a large orange sofa—a curved four-seater designed for optimal television viewing, perfect for stretching out, complementing the sofas with matching chairs, and dark blue curtains draped the windows. In the middle of the room was a large circular dark wooden coffee table.

On the far wall hung a retro clock, in a metallic sunburst design. A side table had a red telephone and a large transistor radio which Father Morgan told me he used for listening to world news and opinions.

He had a gramophone, also known as a record player. Beside it was a small cabinet with dozens of records, including the Beatles and the Rolling Stones. There was also a Corona 3 Typewriter.

In the kitchen he had an electric cooker, fridge, and a fancy Russell Hobbs kettle, which turned itself off when the water had boiled. I was amazed to see a kettle that could switch off by itself!

After having a good look around the house and all the interesting things in it, I quickly dashed to the bathroom, brushed my teeth, washed and went straight into the dining room. The table was already set with food served.

"I hope you're hungry. It's a Full English Breakfast," Father Paul said.

I was introduced to the English breakfast of eggs, bacon, sausages, tomatoes, baked beans, toast with butter, marmalade, and jam, with a large pot of black tea. This was strange to me. Back home, breakfast was usually yam or cocoyam with black beans or eggs on Sunday, or Ogi and akara (bean rolls). That was how I began to adapt to the English way of life.

After breakfast, we took our cups of tea into the sitting room, and Father Morgan brought out the daily London newspaper for me to read.

Afterwards, it was time to wash the dishes and clean up the kitchen.

"I can handle this myself," I tried persuading Father Morgan to let me do everything, but he refused. Eventually, I accepted it, as I couldn't convince him to allow me to take on all the tasks.

One thing that fascinated me greatly was the uninterrupted supply of electricity in the house. We sat down and watched the TV without any interruptions, enjoying a variety of programs ranging from news to soap operas.

After we rested, he decided to take me to the nearby shop where he buys his groceries.

I was stunned to learn that the shops opened early in the morning and closed late at night almost every day of the week. Unlike in my town where we primarily relied on markets that were held every five days, with only a few individual shops that were often poorly stocked. The shop keeper's hours were erratic, and you never knew when he would be there.

On opening the front door, I was intrigued to see the entire front yard and the pavement completely covered with snow. So, we went back into the house and brought the shovel to clear the pathway before we could walk to the street. Most of the neighbours had already been out and shovelled their frontage.

Participating in this activity was fun for me. I could hardly believe that despite the snow and cold, life still goes on. People were working, playing, and moving around as if everything was normal.

We left the house in his car, as the supermarket was a short drive.

The size of the supermarket was staggering. It was unlike anything I've ever seen before, compared to what we have in my hometown. Here, you could practically buy all your groceries and household supplies all in one shop.

It was also strange to see that all the items had prices labelled on them and there was no price haggling as was the norm back home. We did all our shopping and returned home.

On our way home, we noticed the street cleaners working, clearing the snow, and spreading some substance on the roads.

Curious, I asked Father Morgan, "What was the substance the truck was spreading on the roads?"

He replied, "It's a mixture of salt and sand. This helps prevent cars from skidding, allowing the tires to grip the road surface better."

But I couldn't understand the rationale behind spreading salt on such vast roads. Back home, salt is only used for cooking or sprinkling on food while eating, or to preserve meats and fish.

All of this was completely strange to me as someone coming from a hot climate. Additionally, having to wear warm underwear, long trousers and a wool pullover all the time was very unusual for me. This too was very unusual for me.

The following weekend Father Morgan arranged a sightseeing tour of London for the two of us to visit some interesting places. It was scheduled for a Saturday morning. Due to our tight itinerary, we woke up very early to leave the house.

"Dress warmly; we will be outside throughout the whole day," he announced.

We left the car at the house and went by bus to have a good view of London and the surrounding area. It was my first time seeing and riding on a double-decker bus, which was incredibly fascinating. I had never seen this type of bus in my entire life.

When we got to the bus stop, it was chilly. We waited about six minutes before the next bus approached. It was a double deck bus. I had never seen this type of bus before. It was amazing to see this. I was determined to sit on the upper deck so I could see London properly. I was amazed by the amount I saw while sitting on the upper deck of the bus.

In ten minutes, we arrived at the station where the sightseeing tour buses departed from. We bought tickets for the excursion.

Afterwards, the bus departed and our first stop was the Tower Bridge.

"The bridge opens only during the summer period." Father Morgan informed me.

"I would love to see how this giant, magnificent bridge will open." I said eagerly.

"And you will, but not until the weather warms up." Father Morgan replied.

We then proceeded to the Embankment Pier, where many excursion boats were already fully packed, while non-tourists boarded other boats for the day's trip. Then we continued our journey towards Big Ben, to 10 Downing Street, the seat of government, to Westminster Abbey, and then the Parliament Buildings.

Our next stop was Trafalgar Square. Pigeons filled everywhere, probably the highest number I have ever seen in my life.

The pigeons were not scared of us. Back home, no bird will dare come near you, probably because they are hunted. But here, the tourists held out crumbs and seeds for the tamed pigeons, and took pictures with many fluttering birds on their arms, shoulders, and head! It was an incredible sight to behold.

We then left Trafalgar Square for Buckingham Palace. This is the official residence of the Queen of England. We were fortunate to witness the Changing of the Guard ceremony, and there were large crowds of tourists from all over the world. We also visited the Hyde Park Corner and the famous Madame Tussaud's Waxworks.

The contrast was striking compared to my hometown. In London, there are numerous sightseeing activities, whereas in my town, we only have the king's palace, Anglican and Methodist churches, and the Iledi, where the chiefs and kings occasionally hold meetings and traditional worship celebrations.

All of these places are within a 20-minute walk from each other. In London, tourist attractions are spread across different parts of the city, and many of them could easily occupy you for half a day or even a full day.

After a long day of sightseeing, our tour finally ended, and we boarded the last bus to return home.

"Did you enjoy the excursion?" Father Morgan asked.

"Oh yes, the whole day was a lot of fun. What great experiences I had today," I replied.

On entering the house, I was so exhausted that all I craved was a good night's sleep.

We quickly had salad with chicken for dinner, and then I headed straight to bed, where I enjoyed a peaceful and restful sleep.

In the days that followed, as we explored the city, being a first timer, it was fascinating to see that wherever we went, people were already in the Christmas and pre-New Year spirit.

The major roads were embellished with decorations and colourful Christmas lights of different shapes. In addition, the larger shops were decorated with Christmas trees, lights, and creative seasonal window displays.

I was thrilled to see how people embraced this time of the year in London. I could feel the festive mood as I observed people shopping till dusk each day for Christmas presents for loved ones, friends, and family. Others were busy shopping for fancy New Year's Eve outfits.

As Christmas approached, I greatly felt the absence of my immediate family, most especially my wife, son, mother, and father. We're accustomed to spending this period of the year together.

This was the first time we were separated by the ocean. I felt like jumping on the next plane and returning to my hometown. The Christmas feeling was overwhelming. I had many restless nights, and at times I struggled to fall asleep.

At times, Father Morgan could sense that I was thinking about my immediate family and knew that I missed them greatly.

"What's on your mind? Are you still thinking about your family?" Father Paul asked.

"No. No," I lied, pretending everything was alright.

As Christmas Day approached, he bought me a present - the King James Version of the Holy Bible.

We had our special dinner of roast turkey with roast potatoes and Brussel sprouts, fresh tomatoes, and rich gravy on Christmas Eve, 24th of December.

While most English people typically wait until lunchtime on Christmas Day for their stuffed roast turkey, goose or chicken, and steaming plum pudding with brandy sauce afterwards, Christmas dinner was a vastly different meal from back home. There, we will simply have Jollof Rice with beef or chicken.

December 25th fell on a Sunday, and the entire church was packed, much like back home. After the morning service, I returned to the house. Father Morgan still had other church services to attend before returning home.

I went to the kitchen to prepare the meal - Jollof Rice with grilled chicken. When he came back, the food was ready, and I had set the table. We enjoyed our dinner together, engaging in lengthy conversations over various issues till late and then retired to our different rooms for the night.

On 26th December, Boxing Day, there was a significant snowfall which continued till the 27th, with cold temperatures firmly established. By the 29th and 30th of

December, snow drifts reached as high as ten feet in some rural areas I was told. There were reports of easterly gale force winds bringing down power lines, blocking motorways and railways, and leaving people stranded on roads and in trains.

Reflecting about the holiday period at home, I recall how Dad would slaughter a ram and goat early in the morning of the 1st of January. I wouldn't sleep throughout the night, eagerly anticipating the morning slaughter. Dad was the one who typically performed the ritual slaughter of the ram and goat with the help of his relatives.

In the morning, Mum, along with her friends and relatives, would start early preparation of Akara (bean balls), and everyone passing by would be offered some bean balls. In the afternoon, we typically had Ikokore, rice, pounded yam or Ebiripo with vegetable sauce accompanied by hot chilli pepper stew.

In the evening, Dad's friends, the traditional chiefs, would stop by for a visit. For this, chairs were arranged in front of the house, and Dad would have gone out early in the morning to tap palm wine, ready for thirsty visitors.

Prayers were offered to our ancestors for protection, blessings, and good luck for the New Year.

It was a very different experience celebrating New Year's Eve in London.

To capture the atmosphere of my hometown, we attended a service at a church not far from Father's house. The congregation was predominantly African and Afro-Caribbean, with just a few white people in attendance.

I heard some of the church congregation speaking in Yoruba. It was wonderful to hear people speaking my language standing beside me. I was able to speak with them in my own native language, in London.

After the evening service, we welcomed the New Year with great enthusiasm. I felt extremely happy to have begun a brand-new year on the planet in a foreign land. It was truly an unforgettable experience.

Both Christmas Day and New Year's Day were white with the streets and roads covered with snow and chilly temperature. Inside buildings, you hardly felt the cold because there were heaters to keep the house warm. However, as soon as you stepped outside, you felt the harsh biting cold.

Even with a cap on my head, I still felt the cold around my ears. When your ears get cold, they become so numb you can imagine them cracking. My hands also felt the cold, especially when I wasn't wearing gloves. This is why I rarely felt like going outside once I was indoors during the worst of winter, except to buy groceries.

We celebrated the New Year in great style, with plenty of food and drink. It was a lively evening, meant to compensate for not being at home with my family in Nigeria for all the festivities. Father Morgan went out of his way to ensure I celebrated the holiday in grand style.

However, during the holiday period, I also noticed the absence of large family gatherings in London. In Nigeria, we have close-knit family ties, which are deeply cherished. Most of the time, it was just Father Paul and me, indoors.

Back home, people spend most of their time outdoors, except when it's dark. Due to the difference in weather, English people spend most of their time indoors – until spring and summer arrive. In Nigeria, where it's hot year-round, we love being outdoors as much as possible, unlike the Londoners who often sit in front of their electric fires on cooler nights.

Another great thing about home is the frequent social interactions. While in town, you're constantly meeting people on the street, chatting with one person or another, or respectfully prostrating to greet elderly individuals. People greet you with a smile and enthusiasm. But here in London, always surrounded by strangers, I found that sense of community missing.

Here in London, people only greet you casually if they know you, and it's usually brief with either a handshake or a nod.

However, back home, it's forbidden to greet an elderly person with a handshake. You cannot imagine the disapproving looks you will get with that kind of attitude. As a younger person, you are expected to show respect by prostrating—lying down on the ground to greet an elderly person.

January 1963 was recorded as the coldest month of the twentieth century. According to BBC television news, the Straight of Dover, also known as The Channel, was completely frozen over.

February brought more snow, along with stormy winds. However, by the end of March, there were no reports of frost anywhere in Britain. Quite a change…

CHAPTER 8

Studying in England

Right after the New Year celebrations, I began my 'A levels' at the Anglican secondary school in the neighbourhood. This was the school in which Father Morgan helped secure the scholarship.

Father Morgan had been incredibly kind and helpful to me. He even helped in assessing my "ordinary level" certificate, to ensure it met the current British standards.

Excited about my first day of school, I woke up at 5:00 am, feeling eager and unsure of what to expect. After brushing my teeth and taking a bath, I quickly dressed and had breakfast with Father Morgan.

At around 8:00 am, Father prayed with me as usual, and then we both left the house.

Father Morgan sat behind the steering wheel of his Ford Cortina, which he still took great pride in.

"Are you nervous?" he asked.

"Yes, I am, to be honest," I replied.

"Don't worry. Everything will be fine," Father Morgan assured me.

"Amen," I replied.

He drove for about ten minutes, and we were soon at the school gate.

"This is it, student. We are in front of your school. I will come to pick you up at closing."

"Thank you, Father." He then drove off.

I went straight away to register. The receptionist checked the list and came to my name but struggled to pronounce it. She had to screw her lips up in a strange shape in an attempt to pronounce it correctly, but soon gave up.

"Sorry about that, next time I will get it right."

"No problem."

Once I gave her my ID card, I was registered. For my subjects, I chose Economics, Sociology, Politics, and English.

I had relished the dream of becoming a lawyer, even though it seemed like a big undertaking, since no one from my town had ever trained to become one. The idea that I would be the first person to qualify as a lawyer in England and return to my town excited me.

I was shown my classroom, and being the first to arrive, I started wondering where the other students were. After about ten minutes a girl appeared, greeted me, and asked,

"Are you also one of the new students?"

"Yes."

"I am Janet."

"I am Egunbiyi."

Then we shook hands. Other students arrived and joined the class. We exchanged pleasantries and shared a bit about ourselves.

Things went well, and all my initial fear and panic disappeared. A few minutes later, our teacher entered and introduced himself.

"I am Mr. Bryan, your class instructor. To begin, I will take you through the health and safety regulations of the school. Afterward, you will have a chance to ask any questions you may have."

We were taken round the school, and the first day was over. It was pretty good, my first day at the school.

Father Morgan returned with the car and met me at the school gate.

"How did it all go? Did you enjoy your first day?"

"Fine, better than I had expected, as I made some new friends." I quickly got in the car and off he drove. Within ten minutes, we were at the house. We had a hearty banter over lunch, then I proceeded to my room, still pondering about my first day of school in England.

The second day, we copied our daily timetable, and classes commenced properly. I was determined to be studious, as I needed to impress Father Morgan, who had sacrificed so much for me to get this scholarship.

I was resilient about becoming one of the best students in my class. I often studied late into the night to achieve my objective.

Six months later, I began to get deeply fond of one of my classmates, Mary.

Ever since we met at the extra classes organised by our teacher, we had sat side by side, as my desk was next to hers. We were both attracted to and stole glances at each other throughout class. Initially, I was careful of getting involved beyond friendship.

She was adept at mathematics, so I arranged study sessions with her to clarify topics I found challenging. That was how our friendship blossomed.

We would hang out to chat after classes, or at times have lunch together. We would talk at length about the day's studies and the assignments given. Afterwards, I would walk her to the bus stop to catch a bus home.

We finished the first year successfully and were promoted to the second year.

Prior to starting our second year, I secured a part-time cleaning job at a nearby restaurant. The evening shifts, lasting two hours, provided a source of income to help meet some of my financial obligations. Though the pay was meagre, having an income was very welcome.

My friendship with Mary flourished.

One day, I eventually summoned the courage to ask her out.

"Would you like to go out with me for dinner?"

"Where? Which restaurant, and when?" She replied immediately, as though she had been expecting the invitation. We agreed on a date, and everything was fixed.

Before our date, my mind ran wild with different ideas on how to make the date unforgettable. I brainstormed conversation starters and intriguing topics to discuss.

I kept fantasising various scenarios to make it an interesting evening.

Mary and I had our first date at a Chinese restaurant, where we enjoyed delicious food. We had discussions covering various topics, including my family background, her own, my journey to England, and more.

We hit it off splendidly during the date, sharing plenty of jokes that had us laughing until our sides hurt. We enjoyed refreshing orange juice for drinks, followed by a delightful dessert of ice cream.

We finished our dinner, and it was time to settle the bill. I signalled the waiter and requested the bill. It arrived, tucked neatly under a sweet on a plate.

After reviewing the items, I found it amounted to just a couple of pounds. I retrieved the money to cover the cost, but Mary insisted on seeing the bill and splitting the payment.

This came as a surprise to me. Back home, when you invite a lady for a date, the man is supposed to pay for everything. Once more, I observed a significant difference in cultures.

I acknowledged this, though I felt uncomfortable as the one who took her out. However, I appreciated the gesture, as I had just enough to get by at the time.

I walked her to the bus stop, hugged and pecked her. Then, I crossed to the opposite side of the road and caught my own bus back to the house.

The date had been delightful and memorable. Spending the evening with Mary left a lasting impression on me.

After the date, we became inseparable. We often spent extra time together after classes, returning home much later than usual.

She would sometimes invite me for post-class activities, such as sightseeing and visiting museums.

This we did regularly. Mary made me aware that she had mentioned me to her parents as a classmate with whom we did many assignments together.

The month of December and the year-end festivities were fast approaching. This marked my second Christmas and New Year without my immediate family.

On Christmas eve, the 24th of December, I celebrated with Father Morgan. The next day, I was with Mary as she had invited me to her family home for Christmas dinner.

That was the first-time I met with her parents. Her parents were incredibly kind and welcoming, down-to-earth, and easy-going people. I immediately liked them; they were open-minded and had prior interactions with individuals of African descent. Mary's father had worked as an engineer in Ghana, West Africa, an expatriate in the construction industry before returning to England.

He shared stories about how he lived in Accra, the local food and customs, and how he enjoyed his time there. So, to them, it was normal to have a black man as their guest.

For dinner, we had turkey, potatoes, and gravy. Then, we had cake with a cup of tea for dessert.

Mary's parents warmly received me, and I had a pleasant time with them throughout the evening, which was wonderful.

At 8:30 pm, it was time for me to head home. I expressed my heartfelt gratitude to them for the lovely evening. Mary and I walked hand in hand to the bus stop. My bus arrived within five minutes, and after sharing a hug, I departed for home.

Upon arriving home, I found Father already snoring in the living room. My opening of the door must have roused him from his slumber. I inquired why he was sleeping in the living room instead of the bedroom.

"I was waiting for you to return," he responded.

We discussed my evening at Mary's house—how they welcomed me and the delicious meal we enjoyed together. I expressed to him, "What a wonderful evening I had with them." Afterwards, we both retired to our respective rooms. I went to bed still filled with joy, reflecting on my Christmas with Mary.

On the 31st of December, the New Year's Eve, Mary celebrated with her family, while I was with Father Morgan. At the end of the festivities, we returned to school.

This was how our romance began. We were deeply attracted to each other. We kept on attending classes, sharing knowledge, studying together, and preparing for our final examination.

In November, it was time for our final tests, and we approached the examinations with confidence, believing we would perform well. The results were announced, and we both achieved excellent grades. Afterwards, we continued seeing each other.

Whenever Mary's parents were away, I would visit their house. We spent our first night alone after our examination in February. Mary's parents, who were devout Catholics, had gone to Rome on a pilgrimage, a long-awaited opportunity. While they were still in Rome, I visited Mary at their house for dinner, as she had invited me. We enjoyed roast chicken and grilled potatoes with vegetable salad, accompanied by a few glasses of white wine. It was a wonderful evening.

One thing led to another and soon we were in each other's arms, sharing a passionate kiss and making out. We ended up spending the night together, wrapped in each other's arms. In the morning, I returned to Father Morgan's house.

CHAPTER 9

Relationship with Mary

Something unexpected happened after our examinations.

One morning, Mary called me up and said,

"We need to talk."

I sensed something strange in her voice. The voice I heard wasn't the usual Mary I knew. I tried to persuade her to tell me right then.

"Can you tell me what the problem is?" I asked, concerned.

"It's not a conversation we can have over the phone."

All attempts to get her to say another word proved futile.

"Can we meet tomorrow morning at our usual café?" This was close to her house.

With the meeting arranged for the following day, I became restless, with a lot of thoughts flooding my mind.

Is she pregnant? What other reason could there be for needing to meet urgently?

Anyway, the next day, I met her at the little café to discuss her concerns. We sat down to cups of tea and a fruit buna we ordered. I observed her strange, unhappy expression, a sharp contrast to the bubbly Mary I knew.

So, I demanded to know.

"What is wrong, and why do you look so sad?"

Mary searched my face for a while. She was numb, fighting the tears that welled in her eyes. Confused, I handed her a tissue to wipe the tears.

After a while, Mary brought out a letter from her GP and passed it to me. Feeling nervous, I opened with slightly trembling fingers and read carefully. The report said she was three months pregnant! My fears were confirmed. She burst into tears again, and I consoled her. I lifted her face and looked into her eyes, trying to hide my own fears. I asked in a gentle voice,

"So, what are we going to do about it?"

"My parents will kill me if they find out that I am pregnant." Mary sobbed.

A fresh wave of fear washed over me. I shook terribly as I was confused and clueless about what to do next. We had a heated conversation as she had previously assured me that she was okay with being intimate, and nothing would come of it. After a long discussion, feeling unsure of what else to do or who else to turn to, we went our separate ways.

Then thoughts of Comfort and my son back home flooded my mind. As I sat through my journey home, I was lost in thought, shattered by the reality of the mistake I had made. My parents had warned me about the possibility of this happening if I started seeing other girls.

When I called Mary the next day, the only thing she talked about was her morning sickness. She vomited all over the place, and her mother began to suspect something was wrong. Her mother started asking questions about her morning sickness.

"Are you pregnant?!" she demanded in a strong voice on that fateful day.

"Yes, I am!" She blurted out, after making up her mind to confide in her mother.

Her mother was mortified at her response.

She was terrified as she had not had the heart to tell her parents. They expected her to go to university. She hid the pregnancy because her parents were conservative, and being pregnant at that young age would be devastating for them, especially with a black man.

Her mother demanded to know with whom.

"Biyi, the Nigerian boy," she replied.

In an angry voice, she exclaimed, "Not that black boy?!"

"You are so naïve. Now, you must inform your father. It would have been sensible to wait until you are married and much older before getting pregnant, and certainly not with that black boy."

In the 1960s, white girls pregnant by black men faced criticism from both their families and neighbours. Mary's parents, devoutly religious and churchgoers would be scandalised by the idea of their daughter being pregnant by a black man. Such a situation would be met with disbelief and disapproval, as it was widely unacceptable at the time.

During that era, there was widespread hostility and racial bias against interracial relationships between black and white individuals.

Mary announced to me that she was ready to abort the pregnancy since she had confided in her mother. "But I need to buy the abortion pill, and I don't know where and how to get them," she added.

The 1960s witnessed many young girls die while trying to abort their pregnancies. Her mother was petrified on hearing about abortion pills.

Eventually, Mary decided to tell her father about the pregnancy. She summoned the courage that fateful day when her father returned from an outing.

Her father just had dinner and was relaxing on the sofa in the sitting room, watching the evening news.

"Dad," Mary started.

"Yes, Mary?" he answered.

"I have something to tell you."

"Go on."

"Dad," her voice trembling as she struggled to articulate the words, "I am pregnant."

"What did you say?!" he shouted.

She repeated, "I am pregnant."

He was utterly shocked, unable to fathom how his daughter could be pregnant at such a young age. It was certainly not the news he had anticipated.

"And by whom?"

"Biyi, the Nigerian boy."

He was horrified to learn that she was pregnant by me. Her father was deeply disappointed in her, feeling total resentment for her actions.

"You will have to leave this house," he shouted, boiling in anger.

He stormed out of the sitting room and straight upstairs to his room.

The following day, Mary called and requested that we meet again.

She told me her dad is now aware of her pregnancy and about the current situation at her house.

After the meeting, I left for home and found Father Morgan having dinner at the table.

I was restless and unsure of how to broach the conversation about Mary's pregnancy. I allowed

Father Morgan to finish his dinner and have a little rest first.

He observed my distress and left the dining table for the lounge. I quietly trailed behind, requesting for him to pray for me.

Surprised at my request, he said, "What is this prayer for?"

Then I told him I had some disturbing news. He laid his hand on me and prayed.

When he was done, I started, "Father?"

He answered, "Yes, Biyi?"

I summoned up my courage.

"I would like to discuss an issue with you."

"Go on." I stuttered but continued.

"Father, do you remember Mary, my classmate?"

"Yes, I do."

"Erm …erm, she is pregnant by me."

Then I quickly added, "But I will take responsibility for this pregnancy." Father Morgan was shocked as he listened to the story of my affair with Mary, which led to the pregnancy.

I could see the disappointment written all over his face. He knew I was a married man with a child back home. He had expected I'd be more careful in this type of situation.

"Will you go with me to meet her parents?" I pleaded. "Her Dad is about to throw her out of the house."

He reluctantly agreed to go with me.

After a long quarrel with Mary, her parents eventually agreed to meet with me.

Mary, whose relationship with her parents had become extremely strained, was also rattled by recent developments. The atmosphere in her household was tense, with her parents radiating anger and annoyance.

The following day, a Saturday, I went to Mary's house after she had confirmed a time for my visit to her parents. I knocked on the door with great trepidation, unsure of what to expect.

Mary opened the door, and I stepped in with Father Morgan. I introduced everyone. "Please meet Father Morgan, my guardian. Father, meet Mr. Robinson, Mary's father, and her mother, Mrs. Robinson."

This time, her parents, previously friendly and welcoming, now regarded me as an enemy to their family. They gave me a nasty look which sent a wave of panic through my body.

We had a lengthy discussion over the issue. "I'm prepared to accept the pregnancy, though without marrying Mary," I offered.

On hearing this, her father became furious and banged his fist on the table, which terrified me, as I was uncertain about what could follow. In the '60s, it was taboo to have children outside wedlock, and her parents were devout Catholics. After a brief pause, in an attempt to calm the atmosphere, I continued talking,

"I'm prepared to take responsibility as the father of the child," I repeated. "Mary and I can live together as partners," I explained.

Following our extensive discussion with Mary's parents, despite Father Morgan's presence to ease the situation, her father remained adamant, insisting that she leave the house.

After these irreconcilable differences, there was nothing left to say. Father Morgan and I left the house and returned home.

My mind was now preoccupied with how to support myself and Mary. I had to find a full-time job to enable me to rent a flat and have enough for food and other essentials.

I was fortunate to juggle two jobs while still studying: working as a cleaner in the morning and in the evening. This was enough to cover our accommodation and other expenses.

During that period, Mary and I encountered difficulties in finding a place to rent together. Prejudice against us was evident everywhere we went. However, after about a month, I managed to rent a studio flat where Mary and I could live together.

The day I left Father Morgan's house was filled with mixed emotions, as I was embarking on a new life with Mary. It was incredibly hard for me to say goodbye to Father Morgan, who had been a great inspiration in my life.

The time approached for me to part with him. As I drew closer to him for a hug and to bid farewell, tears welled up in my eyes and streamed down my cheeks uncontrollably. Father Morgan noticed my distress and anxiety.

He held me tightly and said, "Let's pray together."

I knelt as he laid his hand on my head to pray for me. Afterwards, I packed my luggage and loaded it inside the taxi already waiting for me.

That was how I parted with Father Morgan.

Mary and I moved into a small, unfurnished studio without any decorations or basics like a fridge, cooker, and a television.

So, we had to do all the buying from a nearby second-hand shop to set up the flat. This was challenging for us, but eventually we moved in and settled down.

As the days passed with Mary and I living together, I noticed a lot of differences in our habits. For instance, I would expect her to always cook and wash the dishes, but she would demand that we share the responsibility.

"The housework has to be shared, including washing of clothes," she insisted. This was hard for me to bear in the first instance, but I had to adjust to it.

One night. Mary woke me up crying due to an agonising pain on the right side of her stomach. At that instant, fear took over; I forgot to breathe and began to run through many what ifs. Praying no harm came to my child or the mother, I regained my composure and called for an ambulance. While waiting, I soothed her and reassured her that everything was going to be alright. I'd never felt so useless, hoping my words could provide some reassurance.

What took only 10 minutes felt like a decade.

When we got into the ambulance with the help of the nurses, the pain seemed to calm down. We arrived at the hospital and the doctors' conducted checks on my wife and the baby. They reassured us that everything was fine, and we had nothing to worry about.

If only that was the case…

After her discharge, she insisted on going to her parents' house. When I reminded her of their strained relationship, she began to shout and curse. Concerned for her well-being after the scare, coupled with her tears, I reluctantly agreed. I remained silent throughout the journey, feeling overwhelmed by the escalating stress, unsure of how to handle the situation.

Upon reaching her parents house, she knocked, and her mother opened the door. Her tears intensified, flowing freely. Mary began to apologise, pleading to be allowed back home. Her mother welcomed her in and as they started to mend their relationship, it became evident that ours was only going to deteriorate further.

Her father was sitting in his living room, and though reluctant to allow her in at first, after a brief explanation from her mother, he irritably allowed her to sit down. She explained to her parents what had happened, and all I felt was a hard glare from her father.

As their hearts softened towards their daughter, they hardened towards me: the taboo father of their grandchild. After each visit home, spending more time with her parents, she would return to me more toxic, like poison personified.

As time passed, her verbal abuse became more severe, sending shivers down my spine as she found new ways to insult me. She constantly belittled me, reminding me of my worthlessness, leaving me consumed by regret. It wasn't like this before... How things had changed. Her attitude was also unbearable. This behaviour was irritating, infuriating, and unacceptable to me. My thoughts became my only solace, and I began to resent the one who once brought me peace.

I began to think about Comfort, my wife back home in Africa. As her husband, she would never dare expect me to do any domestic chores except when I volunteered to help. Even when she was pregnant with my son, she took care of everything.

When my son was about to be born back home, my mother and Comfort's mother were living with her, providing the necessary help and support until well after the birth.

But here in London, it was just the two of us having to manage everything on our own. It was strenuous, and at times we struggled to understand each other.

The time for her to give birth was fast approaching and tension was always high in the flat. It was a completely different situation compared to a woman expecting a baby in Nigeria.

But I endured and put up with Mary because of her condition.

The hour of her delivery approached, and she called to tell me while still at work.

"My water just broke. I think I may be going into labour!" She said frantically.

I immediately asked,

"Have you called the ambulance?"

"Yes, I have," she said.

So, I hurriedly got permission from my manager at work, who, being considerate, agreed to allow me to go be with her. Upon my arrival at her ward, I noticed her parents were already there with her. That's when it sunk in that she had informed her parents before me.

She was in great pain, shouting in distress.

The nurse said her time had not yet come. She laboured throughout the day.

In the evening, she was taken to the delivery room, and I was told I might be able to witness the birth.

This was unusual for me. Back home, men are not allowed to be physically present with the wife at childbirth. You wouldn't even consider asking to witness the birth.

It was taboo. I didn't know what to make of this information at first. On one hand, it would be the experience of a lifetime, but on the other hand, it was taboo.

Eventually, she was wheeled to the delivery room, and I trailed behind. She was pushed in and the nurse said to me,

"Come in and be with your wife."

I was terrified as I asked her, "Are you talking to me?"

"Yes, to you," she answered.

Inside the delivery room, the atmosphere was different. Two nurses were soothing, encouraging and caressing her, telling her to take it easy as it would soon be over. Also present was a midwife and Mary's parents. That was the first time I got to witness childbirth. I witnessed the whole process.

After a short while, one of the midwives urged Mary,

"Push, push, push, so that the baby will come out."

Mary followed the instructions and pushed as directed. She was told,

"Push, again."

She took a deep breath and gave a final push, and I could see the head of my baby appearing.

Within a short time, the baby was out. What a relief it was for everyone present.

"It's a girl," the midwife announced.

The baby did not cry at first. She was cleaned and put on Mary's chest. They asked me to cut the umbilical cord. I panicked since I had never done this before. I summoned the courage and cut it. Immediately after, the baby cried. What an experience. What a moment. A moment of total joy. Both mother and daughter were hale and hearty. I was overwhelmed with joy.

The fourth day, Mary was discharged from hospital along with my daughter. I came to pick them up with a taxi and took them home.

We thanked all the members of staff present at the birth, and were highly appreciative of their specialist skills, and job well done.

We arrived home and began our lives together as a family. Though I was new to taking care of babies, this was an experience and something to be proud of. It brought me closer to my daughter.

We named her Joan. In the beginning, I was hesitant to touch her. She looked like an angel, innocent and tiny. After some time, I summoned the courage and asked Mary to gently place her in my hand.

I could carry her with only one hand. What a feeling to hold and start to carry her. My fears dissipated. Next, I would need to learn how to feed, dress, change her nappies, and at times bathe her. I started practising this after two weeks.

I could not wait to finish the day's work before rushing home to see my angel. After Joan's arrival, child rearing became part of my life.

Despite the birth of our daughter, the tension persisted. We argued over trivial matters, and even simple tasks like feeding our child could lead to disagreements. Our relationship continued to deteriorate.

The relationship was marred by unhappiness, it was more like an obligatory union. Living together became unbearable, feeling like hell.

The cramped studio worsened the situation, as it was too small for the three of us, but I lacked the funds for a larger space.

One fateful day, returning from work; I found the flat was empty. My child, gone, Mary, gone and all valuables were missing. Frantic thoughts raced through my mind as I wondered where she could have gone.

Mary could have gone to her parents I thought. I hurriedly went to Mary's parents' house and knocked on the door. They inquired who was there? and I replied that it was me.

The father opened the door and sternly instructed me to leave and never return. To my surprise, I heard my daughter crying inside, and I saw Mary standing there. Initially, I felt relieved to find them at her parents' house. But Mary's father remained adamant that I leave. I insisted that I won't leave without my daughter. The argument escalated, and a few minutes later, the police arrived.

The police asked who called them, and Mary's mother admitted that she did. They inquired about the situation, and she explained that there was an argument, and that I wanted to break the door to leave. They requested me to leave the property, but I felt unheard and tried to explain my side of the story.

"My daughter is here. I need to be with her," I pleaded.

Despite my protests, I was forced out of their property.

Before I left, I moved closer to my daughter and whispered into her ear.

"I will come back to see you, and you will always have a place in my heart."

It was an agonising moment for me. I could barely stand the thought of parting with my little angel, but the atmosphere was too hostile for me to stay. I feared that if I didn't leave, something terrible might happen. With a heavy heart, I left, sobbing uncontrollably. The pain of leaving my daughter, who was just over a year old, was unbearable.

As I departed, my heart weighed heavily with the thought of leaving behind my beloved daughter, Joan, whom I adored and had grown so accustomed to being with.

Coming to terms with the reality of leaving my daughter at such a tender age was incredibly difficult for me. It felt like a nightmare, as if I were living in a dream that I couldn't wake up from. But it was all too real, a harsh and painful reality that I had to face.

CHAPTER 10

Comfort Arrives in England

The breakup with Mary took a toll on me. It was hard to accept that I would no longer spend mornings with my daughter, Joan, like before, feeding her and feeling her tiny hands while changing her diapers. Although the separation was painful, I had to accept that Mary wasn't the right match for me and move forward.

I finally decided to invite Comfort to England, after getting over the breakup with Mary. Despite the heartache, I remained connected to my daughter, nurturing a strong and loving bond with her.

I sent Comfort a letter of invitation to England, but it took ages before she saw it. I wondered if she had received the letter or just chose not to acknowledge its receipt.

Upon receiving the letter, she was filled with immense joy and disbelief at the news. When she shared the news with my parents, they instructed her to visit Uncle Bayo. She travelled to Lagos, and Uncle Bayo accompanied her to the passport office to fill in an application form for her Nigerian International passport.

Her excitement was palpable as she couldn't contain her happiness. The thought of travelling to England to reunite with her husband filled her with incredible joy.

It was a moment she had never imagined possible—an unthinkable scenario. She travelled to Lagos to meet Uncle

Bayo that took her to the passport office, and this facilitated events.

Two weeks later, she returned to Lagos to collect her travelling documents, in preparation for her journey to England. On getting there, her documents were ready and handed to her. She returned to our hometown to finish preparations before departing for England.

On getting to the town, she broke the news to my parents,

"I got it, I got it. I got my visa to travel. I am travelling to go and meet my husband," she screamed with excitement.

"Congratulations," said my parents.

Do you care to have launch with us? My mum asked. Thank you so much mum, I am full, she replied. She was full of excitement. I need to go now to my parents.

Afterwards, she went to her family to break the news to them. The news spread like wildfire that Comfort was leaving Nigeria to meet her husband in England.

During the summer, I arranged for flight tickets for her and my son to join me in London. Within a month, she would be with me in London. The reality of it all still felt surreal to her. She eagerly anticipated the day of her departure, counting down the hours and minutes until she would finally board the plane. Finally, the day to travel arrived. A chosen few family members travelled to Lagos to bid her farewell at the airport. My parents, her parents, and several other relatives gathered to see her off. They were also bidding farewell to their grandson at the same time.

It was quite unlike when I left Nigeria, where almost the entire town turned out to bid me farewell. That was extraordinary.

The family had hired a bus from our hometown to Lagos for Comfort. Upon reaching Lagos, the time for her departure arrived. She hugged and knelt to greet everyone, bidding them all farewell. Boarding the plane, she travelled to Kano before finally arriving in London.

She arrived during the summer as I didn't want her to experience the winter period, like I did. I wanted her to retain the feeling of the African climate so that both she and our son could gradually acclimate to the cold weather.

Before Comfort and my son arrived, I had rented a studio flat in the East part of London, Hackney. It was a studio in a block of flats. It had no garden, but surrounded by flowers planted in tubs. There were also a few small parks nearby for leisurely strolls.

A day before their arrival, I had gone to the shops to buy some food stuff to stack the house and prepared her favourite dish in anticipation for their arrival. I cleaned the whole house and arranged the whole house properly.

The following day, I left for the airport in the morning. On arriving at the airport I went straight to the arrival lounge.

I waited anxiously at Heathrow airport for their arrival. When they finally emerged from the arrival lounge, I was the first to spot them. Comfort looked much the same, but my son had grown significantly since I last saw him in Nigeria.

"Comfort, Comfort," I whispered, and their faces lit up as they saw me. I couldn't contain my joy at seeing them both. They hurried over to me. On approaching me, she knelt to greet me ass our custom demands, while my son prostrated for me. Afterwards I embraced Comfort tightly before turning to hug my son. We had a wonderful reunion. My joy was immeasurable. It was an unimaginable reunon.

He had undergone a remarkable transformation. He now bore a striking resemblance to me and had grown much taller. It was a moment of pure happiness and pride.

I greeted him warmly, but he seemed quiet and shy. When I asked if he recognised me, he shook his head.

Comfort then explained to him that the person in the photographs she often showed him, whenever he asked about his dad, was indeed me.

"How is everyone back home? Your dad, mum, and your grandparents?" I inquired.

"They're all fine and send their best regards," she replied.

"And how about our town, the elders, and the festivities? I really miss them all, you know," I added.

Despite the bittersweet longing for home, I couldn't help but feel overwhelmed with joy at finally being reunited with my wife and son.

We left the airport and made our way home by bus. Throughout the journey, Comfort wore an expression that hinted at excitement and contemplation about the new life she would be starting. It was a warm day, and the weather made it feel as though we were back home in Nigeria.

After arriving at the last station, we boarded another bus to reach my flat.

Once we got home, I had prepared Comfort's favourite meal - rice, vegetables, and chicken with chilli pepper. She savoured every bite, thoroughly enjoying her arrival.

Comfort maintained her African way of life. Each morning, she would still kneel to greet me with: "Good morning, my husband" as our culture demands.

She took on the responsibilities of homemaking with enthusiasm, cleaning the entire flat, cooking for me, washing the dishes, and even taking care of my laundry and ironing.

She would prepare my breakfast each morning, and by the time I returned home in the evening after work, dinner was ready, and we enjoyed eating together as a family.

I was fully respected as the breadwinner of the house.

Gradually, I started to introduce her to the English way of living and the diverse culture. I introduced her to the traditional British breakfast of toast, eggs, baked beans, sausages, bacon, and a cup of tea.

I registered her and my son with the local GP for their medical care.

She was also amazed by the availability of electricity twenty-four hours a day. Back in Nigeria, our town still lacked electricity, and we relied on lanterns for light. Cooking was done with firewood which she used to fetch from the nearby bush.

Here I had to teach her how to use an electric cooker, which took her some time to get accustomed to.

Now she grinds her pepper with a small pepper blender whereas back home she would grind pepper with a stone.

I also had to show her how to use all the kitchen equipment safely including the electric toaster, oven, electric cooker, and fridge, as she was not accustomed to using any of these appliances. In her kitchen back home, she simply used firewood and a few basic pots for cooking.

The most surprising thing for her was when I outlined our responsibilities in Britain compared to those back home. I made it clear that while I currently manage all the household expenses since she's not working, once she starts working, she'll need to share the responsibility of paying the bills with me right away. This includes electricity, gas, council tax, and telephone bills.

She looked at me in astonishment. In Africa, it was understood that as the husband, I would take care of all the bills as my responsibility.

After she had settled in properly, we paid Father Paul Morgan a visit, as I had informed him of Comfort and my son's arrival. He was overjoyed to see them, recalling their last meeting in Irolu, my village, and now seeing them across the ocean.

"Good afternoon, Father," Comfort greeted as she knelt in respect. My son also prostrated to greet him.

"You are welcome to London," Father Paul said warmly.

"How was your trip? Hope you enjoyed the flight.

"It was smooth and pleasant," she replied with a smile, expressing her appreciation.

"Your son has grown so big that I hardly recognised him. Have your seat." After a lot of discussions, he invited us all to the dining table.

He had prepared Jollof rice and chicken for lunch prior to our arrival, and we all enjoyed a delightful meal together. It was a memorable day for us all, filled with warmth and laughter. As the evening approached, we bid Father Paul farewell and returned home.

During our time in the city, I took Comfort and my son on various outings. One day, we went on an excursion to tourist sites such as Trafalgar Square, where Comfort was amazed to see the place bustling with pigeons. We also visited iconic landmarks like Big Ben, the Parliament Buildings, Westminster Cathedral, explored the shops on Oxford Street and strolled through some of the city's numerous parks. Additionally, we occasionally indulged in trips to the cinema to catch a film together.

After Comfort had settled in properly, I felt it was time to have a serious conversation with her about what had transpired while I was in England without her. I began by revealing to her that I had a two-year-old English daughter named Joan with Mary, my former girlfriend, even though we were now separated. I explained that despite our separation, I had a continuing obligation to provide financial support for Mary and our daughter. To her, it was not totally unexpected, as she is also from a polygamous family -her mother was her father's third wife. So, she took the news lightly, bravely, and with an open mind. She understood the complexities involved and accepted the situation without judgement.

CHAPTER 11

Comfort Becomes a Nurse

Shortly after Comfort and my son, Ayodele, arrived, we reached out to our local school. The head teacher, Mr. Williams, was incredibly kind and led us through the enrollment procedure.

After completing the necessary steps, Ayodele was enrolled at the school, conveniently located near the studio flat I rented for us.

He quickly adapted to the English way of life, as children often do much more swiftly than us adults.

Comfort would wake him up early in the morning and take him to school. At the end of the day, she would collect him and bring him back to the flat.

After a while, he became acquainted with our neighbour's son, James, and they began walking to and from school together.

Comfort was delighted with this arrangement as it allowed her to have more time for herself.

But soon, she began to feel bored sitting alone in the house, waiting for us to return home each day. Back home, she had many neighbours with whom she could spend time, engaging in various activities.

She started to complain about boredom, feeling left alone in the house after we had all gone to our respective places in the morning. And I also knew that after completing her shopping and house chores tasks, she would just sit down and watch the television till teatime.

"Everything is so boring for me. I sit in the flat all day by myself without anything to do!" she exclaimed one day.

"I understand. I am not complaining about your care of the home," I answered.

"I mean, I need to do something else with my life, like working," she replied.

"I do understand how it can be boring sitting alone at home without engaging in any outside activity. I'll speak with one of my married colleagues at work about it. Maybe he might offer some advice about what to do," I answered.

The following day, while at work, I approached Paul, my colleague who happens to be from Ghana, Africa.

"Paul, I have a little problem," I said.

"What will be a problem for a big man like you? Tell me what the problem is," he said.

"My wife is bored sitting alone at home all day. She has been singing at me. You know our women, when they start singing and drumming in your ears, you know there's a problem brewing just behind the doors which will appear soon. To avoid getting bogged down with the problem, it's better to start looking for a solution or acting straight away," I said.

"Haha, tell me about it!" He laughed. "I know exactly what you mean, man. Women are the worst moaners in the entire world, as far as I am concerned. I've got one at home".

"We can only pray to God for guidance on how to live with them, how to know them right down to their fingernails. You are always such a good husband when everything goes their way, I mean, the way *they* want it".

"Once things don't go their way, they don't mind wrecking everything you've worked for. They don't mind driving you naked for them. But they'll tear your finances apart for you if one is not wise with them. Only God knows why he created them in the first place. But we men can't live without them." We both burst into laughter.

"It's biblical. That is why God created Adam and Eve," I replied.

"E no dey easy oo, my brother," he replied in pidgin English.

"Jokes aside, do you know of any jobs she could do for now, something to keep her occupied and stop the moaning? It's really starting to get on my nerves."

"There are jobs like cleaning or packing that we did in the early days when we first arrived in London. If she's interested, they're much easier to find. It's just a matter of going to the agencies, and in the twinkle of an eye she'll have one."

"But I would advise that she consider training for something like nursing, it would be more fulfilling for her, and the pay is much better than menial jobs. After training for four years, my wife is gainfully employed as a nurse now with our general hospital in Haringey.

"What did you say Comfort did before, please remind me," he said.

"She was a primary school teacher back home, and she enjoyed it, especially working with the kids," I replied.

"The best thing then would be for her to retrain and become a nurse. She might work in a local hospital or through an agency when she finishes her studies," he suggested. "After completing her nursing studies, job opportunities are highly guaranteed."

After work, I returned home to find Comfort had already prepared my favourite meal of pounded yam with Egusi (ground melon seed sauce), marinated in dried crayfish and red palm oil, served with cat-fish sauce—a favourite from back home. At the dinner table, I brought up the subject of her going back to school to retrain as a nurse.

"Comfort, I discussed our last conversation about getting you something to keep you occupied with Paul, my colleague at work. He told me his wife is working as a nurse and he believed it would be desirable if you retrain as a nurse. This will give you an opportunity to secure gainful employment upon completion, rather than doing something like working as a cleaner or a shelf packer".

"The prospects of nursing are very good, and you can quickly secure a good job with a good salary upon finishing, working in the public hospitals or through an agency."

But the mere thought of being a nurse made her uncomfortable.

"I hate the idea of working in a hospital. I don't want to be a nurse. I cannot stand seeing blood and helpless sick patients. I would like to continue to be a teacher. I love the idea of working with the kids. That is what I know best," she answered firmly.

Comfort had been a primary school teacher back home, and she wanted to continue in this profession, believing it would better suit her.

The following day at work I told my friend that my wife is still against the idea of retraining to become a nurse. But I still need to have some discussions and convince her.

The following day, upon returning home from work, I once again broached the subject of Comfort attending school in London, as a nurse not a primary school teacher.

However, she was unsure of where to begin, having no prior experience in the field, which I aimed to introduce her to. I attempted to explain to her that she could start as a healthcare assistant, auxiliary nurse, assisting qualified doctors, nurses, and other healthcare professionals in their daily duties.

After undergoing short training, she would gain exposure to various aspects of nursing and could determine what interested her most.

From there, she could decide whether to pursue full training as a registered nurse. If she found that she didn't enjoy it, she would have the option to discontinue her role as an auxiliary nurse.

This she accepted.

A week later, we visited a nearby nursing agency and inquired about the process of getting a job as a health care assistant - auxiliary nurse.

We were told about the responsibilities of a healthcare assistant which included caring for patients at home - such as feeding, bathing, toileting, monitoring vital signs, and measuring blood pressure - as well as providing general assistance in a hospital ward.

We learnt that to start the training, she didn't have any professional qualifications beyond her Nigerian school certificate. However, she would need to take a competency programme beforehand followed by on-the-job training. This was different from the longer-term training required for full-fledged nurses, which typically spanned at least three years of education.

At the time, the training program lasted six weeks. Upon completion, she would be eligible to apply for a job.

She attended the training and the first day proved challenging, as she was not mentally prepared to train as a nurse, a profession she disliked. Nevertheless, she persevered and successfully completed the course.

After completing the six weeks training, Comfort successfully secured a job with the local hospital as an auxiliary nurse. She worked in this role for six months, enjoying a significantly higher salary compared to her previous job as a teacher back home.

However, apart from adjusting to her new job, Comfort faced another challenge— adapting to the cold weather. She struggled to cope with the harsh and biting cold of the winter months, preferring the warmth of hot weather she was accustomed to back home.

Comfort often experienced bouts of depression, grappling with the challenges of her new life. "What kind of life is this, with no immediate family to talk to?" she lamented, voicing her frustrations.

I empathised with her plight, offering words of encouragement. "With time, you will get used to it, and you will be able to conquer the situation," I reassured her.

Despite my attempts to uplift her spirits, Comfort would sometimes burst into tears, expressing her deep homesickness. "I am just so homesick," she would confide, tears streaming down her face.

Once she adjusted to her new life, one day after coming home from work, she said to me, "Biyi, Biyi, you know I have given the idea of becoming a registered nurse a lot of thought, and I would like to do that. I want to further my education and become a fully qualified nurse."

Upon hearing this, I was ecstatic, overjoyed. I had not expected such news. It was the moment I had been waiting for. Despite my immense happiness, I chose not to show it, reassuring her that everything would be fine. I encouraged her to wait and see.

The following year, she applied for admission to the University of London for nursing training and was accepted. She approached her studies with full enthusiasm, which I deeply appreciated and admired. I knew it was challenging for her to juggle everything at once – studying, taking care of our son, and managing the household.

Each day, she woke up early, attended school, and returned home to take care of the house, all while I had to go to work, too. It was an incredibly stressful routine for her, especially since she was accustomed to having relatives and friends around to help back home. The loneliness of her new life in the city weighed heavily on her, and the constant cycle of school and household chores left her feeling exhausted and sometimes devastated. She got promoted to the final year of her studies.

Her final year at university was exceptionally demanding. Alongside her practical and theoretical classes, she had to prepare for exams. Throughout this period, there was hardly any time for relaxation or family life.

Comfort eventually graduated from university after four years of rigorous study. I attended her graduation ceremony, bursting with pride as her husband. On her graduation day when her name was called to come to the podium and collect her certificate, she ascended gracefully. It was a moment filled with pride and joy. She had made it!

After the ceremony, she expressed her gratitude to me for all my efforts in persuading her to return to school and obtain a qualification.

"Thank you very much. You made it all possible for me, by standing by me and encouraging me to forge ahead. May God and the spirit of our ancestors continue to be with you and bless you. I would not have gone so far if not for my prince. You are the man of my life. I am so delighted and happy to have graduated," she said.

She also recalled the challenges she faced throughout her journey to graduation. "Wake up, go to school, come back, and take care of our son and the flat. The same routine every day."

At times she would come home from school extremely tired, feeling totally overwhelmed.

I also reflected on the first day I approached her to consider becoming a nurse, and the reactions that followed.

"Woman, woman, I admire your sweet words you know. Thanks for all the heartfelt statements. Your words make my day," I answered.

She looked at me, moved closer and wrapped her arms around me. Then, she gave me the most passionate kiss of her life.

Comfort and some of her friends had arranged a gathering to commemorate their graduation. I accompanied her to the event, and we both had a wonderful time.

At the restaurant, Comfort was visibly elated, and she kept requesting more alcoholic drinks, which surprised me. I had never seen her indulge like this before.

Soon enough, she became intoxicated, as her tolerance for alcohol was low. I felt uncomfortable with the situation and decided to call a taxi to take us home before things worsened and I became embarrassed.

After graduating from an English university, I could understand the excitement. Thankfully, upon returning home, our son, Ayodele, was already fast asleep, sparing him from witnessing his mother in a drunken state, which could have been quite embarrassing.

She was completely inebriated! The next day, she became sober and constantly requested water to drink to alleviate her dehydration and severe headache.

"I deeply apologise for yesterday's events. I vow to never touch alcohol again. The experience was far from what I anticipated," she expressed remorsefully.

"Don't worry. I understand. It is just one of those things that happen in one's life, most especially when something very exciting happens or you have something special to celebrate. I am not offended," I replied sincerely.

She applied for a nursing job and was fortunate to secure a position at our local hospital Homerton hospital in Hackney, East London, where she had started her initial training.

Upon receiving the job offer, she was overjoyed and elated. This meant not only a stable employment but also a reliable income stream. The prospect of such stability brought her immense happiness.

She was offered a fantastic salary, far above what I earned in two months. Her earning power increased drastically.

Both of us diligently worked and saved every month and decided to get our own home. So, we started to look for a house to buy. After thorough searching, eventually we saw one that we loved.

Having spent all our time in Hackney, East London, it was our clear preference to remain in this part of the city. We held a deep admiration for the area and couldn't envision living anywhere else in London.

Living near renowned landmarks like Liverpool Street tube station and Bishops Gate Station added to the allure of our neighbourhood. Moreover, the frequent bus services connecting us to other parts of London made it incredibly convenient.

After an extensive search, we stumbled upon the ideal residence: a charming three-bedroom Georgian-style house boasting high ceilings, expansive windows, and a spacious garden. Transitioning from a studio flat, the newfound space felt liberating. With some redecoration, we could transform the house to meet our desired standards.

We got a good mortgage and secured it with a down payment. We officially became homeowners! Before we moved in, we did some minor renovations and redecorated several rooms to our taste.

As we moved in, we met our next-door neighbours who saw us carrying stuff into our new house.

"Are you the new tenant or house owner?" the man asked.

"Yes, we are." He quickly introduced himself as Mr. Robinson.

"Would you like me to give you a hand?" He offered.

"Thank you. But don't worry sir; we'll manage," I replied gratefully.

Our next-door neighbours were a courteous and amiable elderly couple, approximately sixty-five years old, as I inferred from their appearance. They had a daughter who was twenty years old. Originating from St. Lucia, both husband and wife exuded kindness and politeness.

"We have lived in our house and in this area for the past ten years. We are fortunate. The neighbourhood is quiet and all who live here know one another," he explained.

That was positive news, the kind one wishes to hear about his new neighbourhood.

After more hearty conversation, we went into our different houses.

We were good neighbours.

Now that we were both earning, we decided to split the cost for the mortgage and all the other bills that needed to be paid.

Shortly after, Comfort received a promotion at the hospital, which meant another salary increase for her. This completely went to her head. A newfound arrogance, coupled with disrespect started to develop in the household as a result.

I got the first shock of my life when I returned from work one day and found my supper wasn't ready. So, I asked for my food.

"Comfort, what about my food? Is it not ready or what?" I demanded, feeling puzzled and a bit annoyed.

"It's in the kitchen," she replied.

"What do you mean in the kitchen?" I asked.

"Go to the kitchen and warm the food. I am extremely tired," she remarked.

I thought she was kidding. I repeated myself and she gave me the same answer,

"Go and make the food yourself. I told you I am too tired."

I couldn't believe what was unfolding before my eyes. It felt surreal, as if this couldn't possibly be happening. Anger surged within me, and I struggled to contain it.

Was this the start of the downfall? The thought sent shivers down my spine, and I knew I had to keep my emotions in check that night, fearing that something dreadful might occur.

It was unfathomable to me that this could be Comfort, my beloved partner. Back in Africa, she would meticulously set the dining table, placing my food alongside my drinking water and a bowl for washing my hands. The stark contrast left me bewildered and disheartened.

I could never imagine Comfort copying the European way of life.

I suffered total humiliation from my African wife who I brought to London.

It was unbelievable.

That night, I resolved not to eat the meal she had left in the kitchen. Instead, I hastily left the house and headed to the café around the corner for dinner.

Upon returning later, my mind was still consumed by the thoughts of Comfort's inexplicable behaviour and the unsettling turn of events for me. As I entered the bedroom, I pondered how I would manage to find sleep amid this turmoil.

Lying beside her, I couldn't bring myself to sleep as we usually did—legs entwined, drawing close, and hugging her throughout the night. I turned my back to her, the distance between us palpable. Eventually, exhaustion overtook me, and I later slept and had nightmares.

The next morning, when she greeted me, I didn't even respond. All I could muster was a disdainful and almost demonic glare. Without another word, I hastily left the apartment early and headed straight to work.

Throughout the whole day at work, I could not concentrate as I wasn't myself. The first solution that came to mind was to stop eating at home altogether and start dining out instead. It seemed like a straightforward way to assert my independence and reclaim control over my home.

Another strategy I considered was to keep cool and snob her when I came home.

I also contemplated the idea of staying out late each day and heading straight to the bedroom to sleep upon my arrival. This would serve as a subtle way to assert my presence while avoiding unnecessary confrontation. Or act as if she didn't exist. Avoid making any contact with her. Maybe all this would do the trick.

I continued to ponder!

Despite the necessity to adapt to changing circumstances, I found myself reluctant to accept this reality.

Throughout my day at the office, I couldn't shake off the weight of the situation. Something had to change; I couldn't simply let things slide.

"I need to teach her a lesson!" I resolved within myself.

On the first evening following our misunderstanding, I purposely stayed out late, ensuring I arrived home after she had already gone to bed. Before returning, I made a deliberate stop at the fish and chips shop to have my dinner before coming home.

She was already asleep by the time I got home. The next morning, she woke up early for work and greeted me. I ignored her. She left the flat before me.

This routine led me to develop an interest in eating fish and chips or chicken and chips, despite my initial dislike of eating out. I stuck to this for a few days, deliberately started coming home late to avoid eating the meals she prepared.

However, whenever she noticed the untouched food, she had made for me on the table the next morning, it made her unhappy.

One day, she attempted discussing the issue with me, but I was not interested in the conversation and ignored her. I needed to show her who the boss is!

She made several attempts to break the ice but saw I was not going to bulge. She decided to seek help from Father Paul.

She went to Father Paul and reported me to him, fully aware he would intervene and address the issue.

Father Paul summoned me to his house, and I explained all that happened between us. The following weekend, he invited both of us over. When we arrived, he led us in prayer, seeking a peaceful resolution to our conflict. After some deliberations, the matter was resolved. We returned home laughing, relieved that peace and harmony had been restored both at home and between us.

However, she gradually grew accustomed to her new routine and lifestyle.

CHAPTER 12

Problems with Comfort

Our son, Ayodele, was soon turning eleven and it felt as though time had flown by. It seemed like just yesterday when he came into our lives, and shortly after, we moved from Nigeria to England to be together.

The idea of expanding our family had occupied my mind for a while. However, I hesitated to discuss it with Comfort, finding it challenging to broach the topic.

I waited patiently, hoping for the perfect moment to share my thoughts with her.

The perfect opportunity came on Valentine's Day. I headed out early to the flower shop nearby and bought a bouquet of roses to surprise Comfort in the morning.

She was taken aback when I presented her with the flowers to celebrate Valentine's Day, something I hadn't done in years. Along with the bouquet, I included a bottle of Obsession perfume and a packet of chocolates as part of the gift.

She squealed in excitement and exclaimed, "For me?" and I answered, "Yes for you my darling."

She rushed over, hugged me, and planted a kiss on my lips.

I was exceptionally gentle and attentive to her throughout the entire day. I consistently asked, "Is there anything I can help you with?"

She couldn't shake off her suspicion regarding my unusual calmness and involvement around the house, but she maintained her composure.

For Valentine's Day, she prepared a special meal for the family. The table was beautifully set for the three of us, featuring a delicious spread of salad, Jollof rice, and grilled Tilapia fish.

After praying, we enjoyed the meal together. Once Ayodele excused himself and left for his room, I seized the moment to open the bottle of wine that had been sitting on the table. Pouring us each a glass, I offered a toast.

We enjoyed a smooth discussion in a relaxed mood and atmosphere with the jazz music playing.

The moment I had been waiting for had finally arrived.

"Comfort, there's something important I'd like to talk to you about," I began.

"Sure, go ahead, what's on your mind?" she replied, her curiosity piqued. My heart pounded with nervous anticipation as I prepared to broach the subject.

"I've been thinking... I'd like to discuss the possibility of having another child," I stated, feeling the weight of the words as they left my mouth.

She paused for a moment, then shocked me with her bold response.

"I don't want any more children. I am satisfied with Ayodele as our only child. May almighty God bless him for us," she said.

"Given our schedules, with me working most of the time and our differing shifts, I don't see how we'd manage with another baby. I wouldn't have the time to tend to nighttime cries, and you wouldn't always be available to help.

I don't think I can cope with another child, with Ayodele nearly a teenager," she replied.

Before giving birth here in England, careful planning is essential. Unlike back home, family dynamics in England typically involve just the woman, her husband, and their children. Life in England differs significantly from the life back home, especially when it comes to childbirth and upbringing. Back home, we have numerous family members eager to assist, including my mother, Comfort's mother, and other relatives. However, here in England, we had no other family support.

After numerous discussions to convince her, Comfort eventually accepted the idea of another child, and we agreed to try for another baby. What a relief.

Unfortunately, our efforts in the first year were unsuccessful. It took us two years of trying before Comfort became pregnant. However, she was unaware of her pregnancy until she visited her GP complaining of flu-like symptoms. When her blood was tested for an infection, it was discovered that she was eight weeks pregnant.

The GP called to inform her. She could hardly believe it.

What a relief and great news for the family. She was eager to inform me but had to keep her peace until I returned from work.

That evening when I returned home from work, we exchanged greetings and I inquired,

"How did your hospital appointment go?"

With a broad smile on her face, she quickly narrated the whole experience to me.

"It went well. Guess what I was told by the doctor," she replied with a twinkle in her eyes.

My mind was not even going to the news about her pregnancy. "You know I don't like the word 'guess,' so please, just tell me," I said.

"Anyway, I am eight weeks pregnant."

"Oh my God, that's fantastic news!" I exclaimed, overwhelmed with joy at her revelation.

I was delighted we would soon be having another addition to the family. It was a big relief. This news called for celebration.

"God of our forefathers, I thank you for our answered prayers. Let all be well with the mother and the new baby. Let us hear the voice of the mother and baby at the hour of delivery. Ase – Amen."

I poured some wine on the floor to signify a drink for the spirits of our forefathers and ancestors. Then I drank the rest at a go.

After going through Mary's pregnancy, I felt more prepared for the experience of a woman's pregnancy in Europe. I had gained valuable insight and knowledge from that previous experience.

This time, I took things easy as I was now aware that in case of any challenges, we could call on the emergency ambulance crew and be taken to the hospital for immediate attention.

Comfort was known for her strong character, especially when it came to handling challenges of this nature.

But due to the significant gap between pregnancies, Comfort found herself frustrated and overwhelmed. She no longer knew what to do or expect during pregnancy and had to readjust to a lot of things.

She struggled with constant fatigue, spending most of her time sleeping. Everything felt different; things seemed to fall apart around her. She felt more nauseous all the time.

Throughout the day, Comfort rushed to the toilet to vomit. She kept a bowl with her in the sitting room for spitting saliva, a habit that made me uncomfortable, but I maintained my composure.

The atmosphere in the house shifted noticeably. I wondered if it was because I had encouraged her to become pregnant, or she's just trying to exaggerate symptoms during the pregnancy. She would make many demands, such as,

"Get me some food."

She turned into a voracious eater; always craving food and snacks. She could wake me up in the middle of the night to prepare her a sausage and bread.

This was not all. "Get me a glass of Pepsi," she ordered once in the middle of the night. Or "Put the TV on. My back is aching."

"I need you to help scrub and massage my back and hold me to stand."

Oh my God! The situation became incredibly challenging and overwhelming for me to bear especially with her constant mood swings.

She would often instigate fights or pick arguments over trivial matters. She would also ignore me for the rest of the evening.

Tasks that she could typically handle by herself became burdensome for her. She constantly criticized me, and eventually became like an agony aunt in the house.

Comfort's sudden aversion to my fragrance, which she once adored, was startling. The mere scent of it now triggered immediate nausea for her. She developed a strong dislike for my perfume.

Whenever she looked in the mirror, she would complain of her beauty fading away. She had gained more weight, her skin darkened, big pimples like a boil, and a widened nose.

There were times when Comfort would forget things quickly, leading to frustrations. She could explode when she expected me to remember details she had mentioned. These were issues we never discussed. She often complained that I didn't listen to her and tended to forget things easily. She overreacted to minor issues. All of this I felt was totally out of order.

Sometimes, she would burst into tears without any identifiable reason, or suddenly become extremely angry.

This type of attitude would not have been tolerated if it was happening back home in Nigeria.

I turned to reading books about mood swings in pregnant women, devouring them in an effort to better understand and handle Comfort's condition and the challenging situation we were facing.

Coping became my main focus.

I had heard stories about women losing their babies due to tense household atmospheres. It was challenging for me, but I knew I had to remain strong and manage the situation as best as I could.

The books provided valuable insights into handling Comfort's condition. It became evident that she was experiencing prenatal depression, compounded by both physical and emotional challenges, as well as psychological issues.

I was counting the days until the nine months would be over. With what I went through daily, the ninth month had better come quickly!

Before reaching the ninth month, we diligently prepared a list of items needed for the new baby's arrival. Starting from the fourth month, we began purchasing baby essentials monthly. We opted for unisex items since it could be either gender.

This time around, there was much more to buy. We bought for the first time a baby cot with a sturdy mattress, complete with sheets and light blankets for warmth. Additionally, we bought baby clothes, nappies, feeding bottles equipped with newborn nipples, burping clothes, baby care products and ointments. This was a lot compared to simpler preparations we made when Ayodele was born in my village, where he was exclusively breastfed.

The joy of welcoming a newborn overseas was also different. I was eager to welcome our child born outside the shores of my country, Nigeria. Children born across the ocean are called Tokunbo – meaning he or she came home from across the ocean. Adetokunbo will be added to his or her name.

One day, during her ninth month of pregnancy, Comfort rang me at work to tell me that she was experiencing some discomfort and would be calling for an ambulance, which she promptly did. She was taken to the emergency department of the hospital, where preliminary tests and assessments were conducted to ensure everything was okay.

She was later transferred and admitted into the maternity ward. After work, I visited her in the ward.

"How are you doing?" I asked.

"I am better now," she replied, a smile lit up her face. We had a light banter, and I returned home later that day.

On the third day, I left work early to be with Comfort at the hospital. This time, I was determined to be by her side for the birth of our child, witnessing the miraculous moment firsthand. It was an experience I couldn't have back home, where it was traditionally forbidden for husbands to be present during childbirth. She was screaming as if she had never experienced childbirth before. She complained of cramps, back pain, and various other discomforts. The midwife came, examined her to determine if her water had broken, but it had not, so she was left to rest for a few hours.

"Rub my head, my hand, and my face," she cried out to me, just like a small child. This was becoming overwhelming, but I remained calm.

"Oh, the pain is there," on touching a particular place. "Oh, now it's moved to another place," as she felt the pain shifting.

She was moved to the delivery room. I followed her straight away.

"The baby is now ready to come. Push, push, push," the midwife encouraged her.

She pushed, and soon the midwife noticed the baby's head and got ready to help the head out. She asked Comfort to give a final push, which she did.

I witnessed the whole process and was also there to encourage her to be strong to push when she was asked to do so.

The baby slipped out and was immediately carried away by the midwife to be cleaned up.

"It's a boy," she announced, then placed the baby on Comfort's chest.

"Take the scissors and cut the umbilical cord," the nurse said.

Once again, I was fearful of undertaking this task. I vividly remember the moment when I was permitted to sever the umbilical cord connecting my daughter Joan to Mary. After some hesitation, I summoned the courage and proceeded to cut the cord. The baby's cries filled the room bringing a sense of relief and joy as we knew the ordeal was finally over. Although Comfort would have loved a girl as our second child, we were grateful for the healthy arrival of our baby boy.

On the fourth day, Comfort was discharged from the hospital. I came with the taxi to pick her and the baby up and take them home. Our neighbours were delighted to see us.

"Congratulations!" they chorused.

Thanks a lot," I replied, beaming with excitement.

On the seventh day, we held a naming ceremony for the baby with Father Paul taking charge. Our neighbours and some friends in the neighbourhood were also present. He was named David Adetokunbo.

The arrival of David brought a different experience from when we had our first son, Ayodele. Back then, in my hometown, Comfort had the support of the entire family; my mother and hers were always there to lend a helping hand. But here in England, things were different from what she was accustomed to back home. This was now affecting her.

Following the birth of our second son, tensions began to rise in the family. Comfort became increasingly stressed out. The everyday conveniences she took for granted back home in Nigeria became unfamiliar luxuries in England.

Without the support of extended family, Comfort had to manage all domestic tasks on her own, except when I was not at work. The absence of readily available assistance left her feeling overwhelmed and frustrated. Life seemed particularly unfair to her at this period.

For her, life could not have been more unfair.

Sometimes she would notice some things out of place in the house, and she would get easily upset about it.

Our relationship worsened; we would have constant arguments over even the most trivial matters.

CHAPTER 13

Moving Out of the Family House

One day, I returned home from work and suddenly, an argument erupted for no apparent reason. Comfort expressed her belief that I didn't support her as she needed, particularly in terms of house chores.

I noticed she had been experiencing sleep deprivation, leading to constant frustration and exhaustion.

Tensions had been simmering in the house for a while. Comfort raised her voice at me, and I responded in kind, escalating the conflict.

Before I knew it, Comfort had called the police.

This came as a shock to me and completely uncalled for, especially considering our African upbringing and orientation.

Back home, a wife would never dream of or dare call a policeman on her husband.

It felt surreal; I was experiencing something I never believed could happen or would live to witness. This was the final straw for me.

Soon, there was a knock on the door as the policemen arrived swiftly.

Bang, bang. "Police, police. Open the door!" They shouted from outside.

I went to the door and opened it. I counted four of them!

"Who called the police?" One officer asked.

"I did," Comfort replied. "My husband is the problem. He tried to smack me because of an irreconcilable problem. I was afraid he would beat me up, that's why I called the police."

I was gobsmacked listening to her.

The policeman asked if I did touch her. I quickly denied the accusation, "No! That is not true! I never laid a hand on her. It was just a minor argument. I'm baffled as to why she felt the need to involve the police."

But all they did was advise us to resolve the issue between us, and they left.

I was livid, fearing something terrible might happen now.

After the policemen left, I shouted on top of my voice, "Have you gone insane? What has come over you?!"

Feeling devastated by the whole situation, I packed my belongings and left the house. I could not believe a girl I brought to London all the way from Africa could do this to me.

Life felt utterly changed for me. I couldn't shake off the feeling of betrayal. Hearing stories about African women changing after coming to Europe was one thing but experiencing it firsthand as part of my own story was another. Comfort had completely lost touch with her African woman's values.

That was how Comfort and I separated.

I checked into a Bed and Breakfast near our house.

Due to the challenges, I was facing in my personal life, I began to encounter difficulties while working as a cashier. I found it increasingly hard to make accurate calculations at the tills, as the figures just wouldn't add up. Similarly, I struggled to handle customer complaints and interact with the irate and impatient ones who glared at me. What used to be manageable before was now becoming overwhelming, and I found it increasingly difficult to cope with these situations.

One day, my manager, who had been observing the sudden change, summoned me to his office.

"What is the problem with you, Biyi?" he asked. "You are a changed man; things are not the same with you. You keep to yourself most of the time now and constantly look downcast. What is going on in your life? You can confide in me; I am your friend, and I sincerely want to help you if it's within my power."

And he was right. At work, I had become a reserved person, keeping to myself each day, as thoughts of my two failed relationships occupied every waking moment. The separation from Comfort was incredibly bitter. I could not imagine that things would deteriorate to such an extent between us. Having no access to my children every day was particularly difficult to come to terms with. It was hard to accept that the family I once took pride in had become dysfunctional.

Consequently, I was in a sour mood most of the time.

When I reflect on how much time and effort, I had invested in ensuring my family's stability, I felt sick at heart. I was allowed to visit the children weekly, but whenever I left them, I became emotional with my heart so heavy that I shed bitter tears. I could not fathom how much things had changed. At work, I was no longer the same person. My colleagues noticed that something was off, and it was evident that I wasn't myself. I found myself making small mistakes every day, unable to concentrate as I once could.

I confided in my manager and told him all that happened to me.

"Why don't you take one week off? Maybe that will cool things down for you," he suggested.

I took the offer. Struggling with depression, I turned to alcohol as a means of coping. I found myself drinking heavily to numb the pain of my situation.

However, during a week off from work, I sought a solution to my troubles. In my search for answers, I stumbled upon a psychology magazine, hoping to find ways to address my problems.

I found several articles on how to deal with emotional problems and read that drinking would never solve the problem but would only make matters worse.

So, my first problem was how to deal with my heavy drinking. I was determined to deal with the situation. I started investing in personal growth and self-help books, to seek inspiration from others who had overcome similar challenges. I read them in my spare time, especially when thoughts of the loss of my family weighed heavily on my mind.

Eventually, I joined a reading club, immersing myself in this new activity. Focusing on reading and personal development helped me gradually overcome my depression and break free from my love for alcohol.

In addition, I made a conscious effort to spend more time with my children, both from my previous relationship with Mary and with Comfort.

This renewed focus on personal growth and family connections played a crucial role in my journey towards healing and recovery.

I arranged outings with them, exploring various attractions around the city. One memorable excursion was our visit to the London Zoo, the oldest scientific zoo in London, which opened on April 27th, 1828. The zoo boasts a diverse collection of over 800 species of animals, including gorillas, mammals, birds, reptiles, fish, amphibians, and invertebrates. The children were thrilled by the experience and thoroughly enjoyed themselves.

We also visited Hyde Park, one of the largest parks in London, established in 1536 by Henry VIII for hunting. Another fascinating place we visited was Speaker's Corner, where anyone could stand up and deliver a speech. Numerous attractive sculptures were scattered around the park.

We made a trip to the Museum of London, which chronicles the history of London from prehistoric times to the present day. Located on London Wall Street, the museum has been open since the 1960s and offers a fascinating glimpse into the city's rich heritage.

I also made a point of taking the children out to eat at various restaurants. It was important to me to break free from the grip of alcoholism and reclaim my life. With determination and courage, I made extra effort to ensure that my struggle with addiction did not define me.

Though the temptation was strong, I remained steadfast in my resolve to be strong for myself and my family.

Over time, my determination began to yield results. I started to think positively that my separation from my family was not the end of my life.

As I started to feel more like my old self, a friend from the office, William, invited me to join him in various activities. We began going to the gym together and engaging in other activities like weightlifting, swimming, attending the theatre or cinema, and eating out.

One evening, after work, I was relaxing and watching one of the English soaps when I heard a knock on my door.

"Who's there?" I asked.

"It's me." It was Comfort's voice.

My mind was in turmoil. Anger welled in me at the sound of her voice. Part of me wanted to ignore her completely and refuse to answer the door. Yet, amid the chaos of my emotions, a rational voice urged me, *just open the door and listen to what she wants to say. What if it is something to do with the kids, or something else that is important...*

I summoned the courage to open the door.

"Yes? Can I help you? To what do I owe this unexpected visit?" I queried.

Comfort knew where I lived as I had earlier given her my address; in case she needed me urgently on matters affecting the children.

"We need to talk. Can you please listen to me," she asked, in a soft repentant voice which caught me off guard.

At first, I thought it might be some sort of joke. However, she greeted me with genuine warmth, a sharp contrast to her previous behaviour. I stepped aside to let her in and returned to my initial position.

She came up to me and knelt down, her face showing deep remorse, as she earnestly begged for forgiveness.

"Your children miss you. I also miss you and your affection," she said.

And added, "The house is not the same since you left."

I listened to her, my mind reeling with disbelief. It felt surreal, as if I were watching a scene unfold in a movie or experiencing a dream.

Yet, amid the shock, a glimmer of hope flickered within me. Perhaps this was an opportunity to mend the rift between Comfort and me.

It would be so wonderful to reunite with my family, especially the children. During our time apart, I had really missed them. Despite my earlier attempts to reconcile with Comfort at the beginning of the crisis, she had refused to listen.

This time, Comfort was more receptive. I couldn't pinpoint what had prompted her change of heart, but I was prepared to set aside my grievances and forgive her.

As she apologised, tears streamed down her face. Initially, I wondered if her display of emotion was genuine or just phony crocodile tears, but on second thought, I felt that her willingness to apologise indicated genuine remorse; she truly meant it and was sincere in her intentions.

We engaged in a heartfelt conversation about our failed marriage and explored ways of resolving our issues. I did accept her apology. She wanted me to move back to the family home immediately, that day.

"Comfort, getting things back to normal between us will be gradual," I said, and she accepted it.

I promised to visit the family that weekend.

As the weekend approached, I found myself in a dilemma of whether to honour the invitation or not. I questioned whether I had acted too hastily in accepting Comfort's apology. Perhaps I should have waited longer before making any decisions.

Despite my initial hesitation, I eventually calmed my nerves, got dressed, and made my way to Comfort's place.

As promised, I returned to the family home over the weekend. The moment I stepped through the door, my heart swelled with joy at the sight of my children's beaming faces. "Daddy! Daddy!" they exclaimed in excitement, rushing towards me with open arms. It filled me with immense happiness to be reunited with them in the comfort of our own home once again.

The enticing aroma of delicious food greeted me as I entered the house. Comfort had outdone herself in the kitchen, preparing a feast fit for a king. The table was adorned with all my favorite dishes: pounded yam, spinach, assorted vegetables, goat meat, smoked fish, and roast chicken. It was a spread that left nothing to be desired. The table was full of tasty, assorted foods.

Sitting together as a family once more, we shared a meal just like we used to in the past. It was a comforting and familiar ritual that filled me with joy. Comfort knew the way to my heart was through my stomach, and her efforts to prepare my favourite dishes did not go unnoticed. The evening was filled joy and happiness as we came back together as a family once again.

Gradually, I began to move back into the house, and the children's happiness at having me home was palpable.

Comfort and I started to work on reconciliation and rebuilding the broken relationship from scratch.

The trust was broken, and it would need time and effort to rebuild it.

Sitting down together, we had candid conversations about the issues that had led to the breakdown of our marriage. Both of us acknowledged our mistakes and made a mutual commitment to self-reflection and improvement. Our goal was to create an environment of peace and understanding within our home once again.

We must learn to accommodate each other's opinions, adopting a policy of give and take, and showing respect for each other.

We resolved to make things work between us.

Taking things day-by-day, we began to address issues as they arose and made tangible improvements in our relationship and daily routines.

CHAPTER 14

Graduation Day

My aspiration of becoming a qualified lawyer in England never wavered. The idea of becoming a lawyer was fascinating to me - a career where I can improve the lives of others and witness the dynamics of human relationships for justice and an egalitarian society.

I was convinced that studying law would help me reorganise my society and maintain law and order.

Secondly, I couldn't shake off the fact that I could be the first qualified lawyer in my hometown. This thought continued to occupy my mind; the dream that I would one day make my family proud and leave an indelible mark in history.

I firmly believed that one day my long-awaited dream would come true.

I was fortunate to gain admission into the London City University of Law to study law. After obtaining an LLB (Hons) law degree, my plan was to become a general practitioner. Following that, I would acquire a license to practice in a particular area of law. I had the option to pursue either the Legal Practice Course (LPC) or the Bar Professional Training Course (BPTC) to qualify as a solicitor.

Constitutional law was my area of interest. This field deals with defining the various entities within a state, including the Executive, Legislative, and Judiciary branches. It also encompasses human rights, statutes, case law, and the conventional rule of law, along with the principle of separation of powers.

For five years, I dedicated myself to pursuing my dreams and I was overjoyed when I finally graduated.

However, achieving this milestone wasn't without its challenges. I had to juggle my studies with part-time work, a task made possible by the understanding manager at my Woolworths office. Despite committing to full-time education, he allowed me to work part-time shifts that fit around my classes, for which I was deeply grateful.

Studying while working part-time was no easy feat. I poured my heart and soul into my studies, often burning the candle at both ends. It was a demanding and hectic period of my life. Balancing the financial responsibilities of supporting my family, endless bills, and a mortgage, all while enduring the harsh winters in England, added to the difficulty. Yet, despite the challenges, I persevered.

That was my student life in England.

There were times when I took on weekend shifts as a shelf-filler at Woolworth's store to bolster my finances and cover my expenses. My focus was solely on working hard and excelling in my studies. Socialising took a backseat as I was driven by the urgent need to make ends meet.

Comfort also played a significant role by contributing a portion of her monthly income to support our family finances.

I cannot believe how the time flew. Before I knew it, I found myself in the final year of my studies, eagerly anticipating my final exams. With determination and hard work, I successfully passed my exams with flying colours. Finally, the day I had long awaited arrived - the day of my certificate presentation.

For the special occasion, I had invited Father Morgan, my wife Comfort, and our two boys. It was the proudest day in my life. The event would always be a cherished memory.

I woke up bright and early in preparation for my big day. I left the house with my family for London City University of Law. I was determined not to miss any part of the event.

I first dashed to the decorated graduation hall, where the event was taking place to take in the atmosphere. Then I registered and received the graduation gown and cap, which I had paid for in advance.

The ceremony commenced promptly at 10:00 am as scheduled. It was slated to be a three-hour affair for all the graduating students. When the hour came, we made our way to the hall and took our seats.

The hall was also occupied by the chairman, vice chancellor, and our guests, who sat in a separate row in the hall eagerly awaiting the moment when their loved ones would receive their certificates.

The vice chancellor began by enlightening us of our roles as new graduates in society. Subsequently, each of us was called to the stage, to collect our certificates based on our seating arrangements in the hall.

At the turn of the law department, we all lined up, one by one. I anxiously awaited my turn. When I heard my name called, I moved swiftly and confidently toward the stage to receive my certificate. I was extremely joyous and happy.

Being the third person called to receive my certificate, the moment felt incredibly special, beyond words.

It dawned on me that this was the most significant day of my life.

With my head held high, I approached the vice chancellor. He congratulated me, shook my hand and presented me with my certificate.

I looked towards where Comfort and my children were seated with Father Morgan.

It was a moment filled with immense relief and joy for me and my family. In that instant, I felt a deep sense of pride knowing that I had made my family back home and the entire community proud. I had finally bagged the Golden Fleece.

After the ceremony was over, the reality of my graduation began to sink in. It wasn't merely a dream, but a tangible reality. I had become the first person from my village to graduate from a United Kingdom university. What a proud moment.

This day will forever hold a special place in my heart, a cherished memory that I will carry with me throughout my life.

Saying goodbye to my friends, with whom I had shared the past five years, was emotional. Although it marked the end of our time together, I knew that some of them would remain a part of my life in the future. Nonetheless, I would miss them dearly. It was so emotional for all of us to be parting. I would miss them greatly.

After the ceremony, Comfort bought a bouquet of flowers from the university shop to congratulate me. She presented me with the flowers and gave me a heartfelt hug and a kiss. Father Paul and the children also expressed their joy and congratulated me.

The photographer captured several moments during the graduation ceremony. Initially, he took pictures of me alone, proudly displaying my certificate. Then, there were photos with Comfort, the children and Father Morgan. Later, we took pictures with my graduate friends.

At that moment all I wanted was to be home in Nigeria again. All I could think about was booking the next available flight, and dancing around my hometown, celebrating this wonderful achievement, proudly displaying my certificate as a qualified lawyer for all to see.

The entire town had been praying for this moment. I wished I could share the joy with my father, mother, and the entire community of my hometown, Irolu Remo.

In the evening, Comfort, my children, Father Morgan and I went to a Chinese restaurant for dinner to celebrate. I ordered the house-special, my favourite, while the children wanted fried rice with prawns, likewise Comfort and Father Paul. As we settled down, Father Morgan led us in prayer before the meal.

"Dear Lord, we come before you with hearts full of gratitude for guiding Biyi on his journey to becoming a lawyer. Thank you for granting him wisdom, knowledge, determination, motivation, and confidence throughout his studies. As he embarks on this new chapter of his life, we ask for your continued blessings and success to accompany him.

May the Holy Spirit be a constant presence in Biyi's life, guiding his steps and illuminating his path. We pray for his safe return to his homeland, filled with good health and prosperity.

We also lift up Biyi's wife and children to you, Lord. Grant them peace and harmony in their lives, and may your divine protection surround them always.

In the name of the Almighty Father, Son, and Holy Spirit, we pray. Amen."

We all chorused, "Amen."

"I am so proud of you on this great occasion. You have achieved the Golden Fleece. Now you can hold your head up as a lawyer from England. I am sure the whole town will be so proud of you on your return home," he remarked.

"Thank you so much, Father. Without you, I would not have been able to achieve all I have today. You supported me and gave me the courage to forge ahead despite my background. I am so grateful to you. There is no way I would write my history without you. You are a blessing to me. Knowing you is one of the best things in my life," I replied.

We all enjoyed the evening. After the celebration, I called a taxi to take my family home, bidding farewell to Father Morgan.

He was the one who ignited my aspirations back in Nigeria, fueling my dream of becoming the first lawyer in my town.

Unable to simply jump on a plane and return home, I began contemplating the necessary preparations for our eventual journey back to Nigeria. After the graduation, I approached Comfort to discuss our plans and the steps we needed to take to prepare.

"Comfort, we should start listing all the things we'll need to prepare for our return to Nigeria," I suggested.

"We already have most of the essentials like fridge, cooker, television, settee, iron and our kitchen utensils. So, what else do you think we should add to the list," Comfort replied.

"I believe I only need a couple of suits and shoes, but I don't know about you," I said.

"I think I will also need a couple of dresses and some more clothes and shoes for the children," she said.

"What about gifts for our parents and families?" she demanded.

"Oh my God, this is going to cost us a fortune; you know we have a lot of families and friends to give. Unfortunately, we cannot give everybody a gift, but we will do our best."

We put our heads together and came up with a plan to leave London in a year. We needed time to save up enough money and make all the necessary preparations for our return to Nigeria.

Right after our discussion, we began our preparations.

I could hardly wait to return home to Irolu Remo, Nigeria, the land of my ancestors, to be among my own people.

CHAPTER 15

Comfort Took Il

I found myself anxiously counting the months, days, hours, and minutes until our departure from London to Nigeria. The idea of boarding the plane and reuniting with my kinsmen consumed my thoughts.

Each morning, I woke up still in disbelief that I had achieved my aim of qualifying as a lawyer - the Golden Fleece. The reality of my accomplishment was a constant presence in my mind. I had become a lawyer.

As I anticipated our return to Nigeria, my focus shifted to practical matters. I began considering how to increase our finances to afford the journey and settle back home. Additionally, I pondered on gaining work experience with a legal firm.

Gaining legal work experience in London would significantly boost my curriculum vitae when seeking employment opportunities in Nigeria.

There were several options available for gaining the necessary work experience. So, I began applying to some solicitor firms in London and fortunately, I secured a part-time position with one of them. Concurrently, I continued my evening job as a cashier at Woolworth in Hackney. So, I did the two jobs.

Comfort and I both worked hard for over a year to ensure we saved enough money for our resettlement in Nigeria.

We had other bills to pay, but we could meet our financial obligations together.

We aimed to live comfortably upon our arrival back home equipped with essential domestic appliances like double door freezer, television, cooker, CD players, etc.

To facilitate our plans, we put our house in Hackney, East London up for sale, anticipating offers from interested buyers. Selling off the house was crucial to pay off the rest of the mortgage and raise more funds for our departure.

After months of waiting anxiously without any updates from our estate agent, we had nearly given up hope of selling the house quickly.

Then, unexpectedly, our estate agent contacted us one day with news that a potential buyer had shown interest in our property.

Learning this brought immense relief as it indicated a possibility that our house would indeed be sold.

Unfortunately, after a series of negotiations, the conditions for the sale were not met, and the house remained unsold. But we kept our fingers crossed that at some point in the future the house would be sold.

However, we found ourselves needing to stay in London for another year to allow me to accumulate sufficient legal work experience.

Despite this change of plans, we remained optimistic and began preparing for our eventual departure. However, one day I returned home exhausted and starving after a particularly busy day and told Comfort that I was ready for dinner.

"Comfort, can you please make my dinner now," I asked.

"Oh, I already prepared your meal. I just need to warm it. Give me a few minutes," she responded.

As she rose to head to the kitchen, I remained seated, watching the television to pass time. A few moments later, a loud crash echoed from the kitchen, the unmistakable sound of plates shattering against the floor.

I shouted, "Comfort! Comfort! What is it?" Rushing to the kitchen, I found her lying prone on the floor, her head wedged between the dining table and the cooker.

Shocked and speechless, I panicked as I struggled to comprehend the situation. Comfort had never shown signs of illness that would lead to her collapsing on the floor. Dread crept in as I feared the worst outcome - was she dead? God forbid.

"Comfort, please answer me!" I pleaded, my voice trembling with fear. The children, alerted by my frantic shouts, came out of their rooms, and saw their mother on the floor.

Bursting into tears, they started shouting, "Mum, mum, stand up." I remained in a state of confusion uncertain about the next step to take. My brain froze as I grappled with the situation. After a few moments, I managed to gather my thoughts and swiftly called for an ambulance.

Our neighbours also rushed to help, visibly shocked by the sight of Comfort lying on the floor. I frantically explained the situation to them, my voice trembling with fear and concern.

"It's my wife," I cried out, tears streaming down my face. "She collapsed, and she's lying on the floor. I'm afraid she's dying."

At that moment, the thought of losing my wife, the mother of our two beloved children, was unbearable. She was not merely my partner, but someone so dear to me; the woman with whom I suffered to get to this stage.

As I knelt by Comfort's side, overwhelmed with grief, I couldn't help but question the sudden turn of events. All our plans and dreams seemed shattered in an instant.

"Comfort, please don't leave me like this," I pleaded, my voice choking with emotion. "The children and I love you dearly. I cherish all we have built together, the children and our struggle for a better life."

Amid desperate sobs, I began to pray, "Oh my God, come to my aid. The spirit of our forefathers, do not leave us nor forsake us in this moment of need."

Before long, the ambulance arrived, and I swiftly opened the door for the medical team to enter.

"What happened?" one of them inquired, their tone urgent and concerned.

"It's my wife, she went to prepare dinner, and suddenly I heard a big thump and plates crashing. I rushed to the kitchen and found her on the floor."

I quickly led them to the kitchen where she was still lying on the floor.

They asked what she was called. "Comfort," I promptly replied.

"Comfort! Comfort!" they called out urgently.

Gradually, she started to respond, softly murmuring, "Yes?" as she slowly opened her eyes and glanced around, trying to understand what was happening. As she attempted to rise, they gently restrained her.

"We must carry out some tests first, so stay still for a few more minutes."

One of them shone a light in her eyes to check for concussion, while another strapped a band around her arm to check her blood pressure, oxygen level, and pulse. Then they checked to see if any bones were broken. Once they had done the necessary examination, they helped her get to her feet, very slowly.

"You don't seem to have suffered any serious injuries from the fall, but we will take you to the hospital to run more tests, to determine the cause of this," the head of the medical team explained to her.

Oh my God, what a relief for me and the children that she had returned to us. I gave thanks...

"Oh, spirit of my forefathers, you did not forsake me. I give thanks to you and the Almighty."

She was quickly placed on a stretcher and carried into the ambulance.

I asked our neighbour's wife to help look after our two boys, as I followed Comfort to the hospital.

The siren as well as siren lights were on during the ride. It took only five minutes to get to the local hospital, as it was near our house. On arrival at the hospital, Comfort was taken to the accident and emergency department where other tests were carried out on her.

I remained by her side for as long as I could, and waited in the visitors' room when they took her away for further tests. I wanted to ensure she was okay before I left.

It was almost midnight when I returned home. I appreciated the neighbour for taking care of my children, and she returned to her own home.

The following day, I went to see Father Morgan, to explain what had happened to me and my family. He accompanied me to the hospital to visit Comfort.

As we entered her room, Comfort laid motionless in bed. Father Morgan gently inquired, "Comfort, what is wrong?" Barely acknowledging his presence, she remained still. With solemn reverence, Father Morgan joined me in prayer by her bedside.

"Lord, I commit your child Comfort into your hands. Let no evil befall her. Guide and protect her. Grant her a quick recovery. Remove her from danger and shower your healing blessings on her at this moment, we pray."

We both said, "Amen."

Later, Father Morgan left us. I remained with Comfort for the rest of the day.

I could not believe how my world was collapsing around me. It was an overwhelming sorrow!

The next day, I returned to the hospital, this time accompanied by our children. To my relief, Comfort seemed more alert and responsive with some energy. Soon, we were all chatting and reliving the memories of our cherished moments as a family. Comfort underwent numerous tests administered by various doctors, seeking answers to the mystery of her sudden collapse.

On this day, Dr. Doddy, a tall, handsome, charismatic consultant, with a pleasant smile, was carrying out an examination.

He carefully lifted her gown and gently probed both of Comfort's breasts. In a gentle voice, he informed us that she would require one more test known as a CAT scan.

She was then taken away to the radiology department and had the scan. It showed a lump in the left breast. This was confirmed to be a tumour. Although, she had received a yearly mammogram a few months earlier, which had not detected any abnormalities.

Hearing the word "cancer" threw me off guard and into deep despair. I sensed Comfort's time was drawing near. The moment you receive a cancer diagnosis, the entire world seems to crumble around you, with everything unfolding at lightning speed.

Cancer, a ruthless and merciless affliction upon humanity, offers no reprieve. Comfort would now have to endure the grueling ordeal of chemotherapy.

The next day, Dr. Doddy, the consultant, arrived with the results of the CAT scan. As he presented the chest x-ray and the scan, we awaited the news anxiously, our heads hung in anticipation.

Dr. Doddy adjusted his glasses, perching them low on his nose for a clearer view. He then held up the x-ray, using a pencil-like stick to indicate the pertinent areas.

"If you examine closely," he began, "you'll notice a dark mass here, resembling a shadow on the breast. That is the tumour. Unfortunately, there are multiple tumours present, and it appears to be cancerous. It has proliferated rapidly throughout your left breast, displacing most of the healthy cells."

The news hit us like a thunderbolt. It was the epitome of bad news, the devastating kind. I felt as though I was in a trance, but I could feel my heart pounding with fear.

Comfort and I spoke at the same time. "Are you *sure* they are cancer cells?"

Dr. Doddy replied, "We must get in there before we can tell you exactly what it is." He promptly recommended a biopsy, a relatively simple procedure involving the insertion of a needle into the breast to get a sample of the tumour cells.

"Then if the results show cancer, surgery will be the next step, to ascertain just how far the cancer has spread, and see whether it can be removed."

Oh my God, my heart was pounding fast. *Maybe this is the end of everything. Now the children and I will lose her, someone I love dearly.* I felt so sorry for her. She was so distressed.

Comfort fell silent and couldn't utter a word. After a few minutes she muttered, "What terrible news. This is a very bad day for me. Breast Cancer means death."

Dr. Doddy went on, "We will do the biopsy this afternoon, and then, if necessary, we will perform an operation soon afterwards. If it is cancer, she will need to be operated on as quickly as possible."

About an hour later, another doctor came in, drew the curtains around Comfort's bed, and asked me to leave while he performed the biopsy. I heard her wince for a second as the needle went in to dull the pain, but it was soon over.

Then I went to have a much-needed cup of tea, while we await the results of the biopsy.

"I am so sorry, Mrs. Egunbiyi, but the biopsy did reveal cancerous cells. Now, the next step is surgery to determine just how far it has spread, and whether we can remove it surgically, or whether radiation would be a better course of treatment," the doctor informed us.

Comfort went pale, "Am I going to die? Please do all that is in your power to save me. I need to be back with my parents, family, friends, and all the town people in my home in Nigeria. Oh, dark days!"

She then burst into uncontrollable tears. I put my arm around her to console her, and then I, too, began to cry with her.

Dr. Doddy implored us not to panic. "We will do everything we can, and hopefully the operation will go well. I cannot guarantee everything will be fine, but I remain optimistic."

Eventually, we both managed to calm down, and as he left, we were left pondering what fate awaited us.

The night before the operation, I gathered the boys and Father Morgan, whom I had briefed about the situation, to visit Comfort and offer her reassurance.

Father Morgan prayed with us for the success of the operation and for Comfort's recovery.

CHAPTER 16

Comfort Admitted to the Hospital

The following morning, the day of Comfort's operation, I woke up around 4:00 am, unable to sleep any longer. Throughout the night, I had been plagued by nightmares. I started praying that all should be well with my wife.

I tossed and turned in bed consumed by questions. What if there were complications, or the inevitable? God forbid any harm befall her. Spirits of our forefathers do not forsake me now!

I bathed and had a leisurely breakfast attempting to distract myself with some reading. However, I found myself reading one paragraph over and over, unable to concentrate. My mind was too preoccupied with worry to absorb any information.

At 6:00 am, I went next door to my neighbours, explaining the situation to them and asking them to look after the boys for the day, including taking them to school and picking them up afterwards. They were sympathetic and understanding, readily agreeing to help.

I took the bus to the hospital, arriving at 6:30 am. Comfort was still sleeping but despite it being before visiting hours, the nurses made an exception due to her impending operation and allowed me to see her.

As the operation wasn't scheduled until the afternoon, I wanted to spend the morning with her to help her feel at ease. I was the one who woke her up.

"Good morning, my darling. Hope you had a good night's sleep." I whispered to her.

"Good morning," she replied, stirring to the sound of my voice. "It would be nice to have breakfast together. But I can't eat or drink anything until after the operation. The nurses informed me of that last night."

The doctor returned not long after, bearing a consent form for both of us to sign. It detailed the potential risks, including complications or even death during the operation, and was meant to protect the hospital from potential legal action in case of unforeseen circumstances.

After signing the form, the doctor explained the procedure of the operation to us.

"The operation we will perform today will initially be exploratory surgery, to examine the extent of the cancer in the breast by removing some tissue from the tumor during the procedure. This will help us determine the stage of the cancer and how far it has spread."

"If the cancer is in an advanced stage," the doctor continued, "we will proceed to remove it immediately. This may involve either a partial or complete mastectomy, which entails removing the left breast along with some of the lymph glands in the armpit."

Upon hearing that the left breast would need to be removed, she became depressed, "But on the other hand," she said, "I am not planning to have any more children. If this will improve my health, I am willing to let it go."

"There might be some bleeding, which should not last. And you may have a bad response to the anaesthetic. You may also experience nausea after the operation, but this should pass soon.

If we do need to remove the breast, we can provide an artificial one later once you've healed from the surgery. Let's take it one step at a time, shall we?" the consultant said gently.

Both Comfort and I signed the consent form.

Later, the anaesthetist arrived to explain how the anaesthetic worked and what to expect. We signed the consent form from the anaesthetist as well. Before the operation, a ward nurse checked Comfort's blood pressure, pulse, and oxygen level and also checked if she was diabetic.

Comfort kept visiting the toilet, while we waited for the hour to come. I wasn't sure if it was fear or panic that was troubling her bladder.

Just before noon, the porters arrived and wheeled Comfort to the theatre.

As we approached the operating room, she looked at me and held my hand tightly, tears in her eyes. I was much stronger this time.

"Don't worry, everything will be fine. Remember what Dr. Doddy told you," I reassured her. She was then wheeled into the operating room, and I was smiling at her. She bravely returned the smile and was gone. The anaesthetic gave her the required dose and immediately was wheeled to the operating theater just by.

After the operation, which lasted over 4 hours, she was taken to the recuperating ward where she spent another 3 hours before been wheeled back to her ward. She was astonished to still see me waiting for her. She thought I had left for the house and will come back probably in the evening or the following day. She told me that once in the theatre, she was hooked up to an IV by the anaesthetist and started to deeply relax.

Before she fell asleep, she remembered seeing medical staff all around her, dressed in surgical green gowns and masks, with various machines beeping on and off. That was all she recalled.

"Afterwards, I opened my eyes. The room felt so cold. *Comfort, wake up*, a nurse said to me.

"I could hear a voice, but it felt distant, unreal. When I opened my eyes, I found that I was being wheeled down the long corridor, back to the ward but to the recuperating ward.

"Then I remember being given pain pills, oxycodone, which the nurses would bring me whenever I pressed the button by my bedside. But I was told to take them only when I felt pain, as they could be addictive."

As she narrated all this, she was already dozing off.

After the operation, she was tired and quite weak for a while. She slept for two more hours. I sat by her side until she woke up and regained consciousness.

The nurse came by and asked her if she was feeling any pain.

"What is your pain like? Can you describe it, by giving me a number between one and ten?"

Comfort answered, "Eight." The nurse gave her more oxycodone.

Comfort enjoyed pressing the button for oxycodone even whenever she felt a minor pain.

After the operation, that afternoon and evening, the nurse came every twenty minutes to check on Comfort.

Then her doctor appeared at her bedside, to see how she was doing. Dr. Doddy asked, "How are you doing? You are a brave woman to have gone through such an operation. Well done."

For me, it was terrifying. The question of whether she would survive or not kept lingering in my mind.

The next morning, Comfort was motionless. She was just staring at her chest, where the breast had been removed. Then she touched the place. It was now flat and covered in bandages.

I stared at her chest. The breast was really gone.

The question she kept asking was, "Why me? It's not true! I can't believe this. What has happened to me?" Denial...

The nurse came to check on the site of the operation, to clean it, put cream on it, and re-bandage it.

She asked if Comfort had gas or passed wind after the operation. Comfort replied, "I sure did!"

Comfort's condition started to improve day by day.

The third day, Comfort could move around her room on her own.

The nurses were pleased with her progress and encouraged her to do more movement and walking around the ward.

My son would walk around the room with her. "Go on mum," he'd say, giving her the moral support she needed.

On the day of her discharge, I arrived early to pick up Comfort. She had already had her breakfast and was eagerly awaiting the doctor's ward visit. When he arrived, he confirmed she had made massive improvement.

Comfort couldn't contain her happiness. She was thrilled at the prospect of heading home.

The doctor also advised her, "Comfort, your life is going to change. You will need to take daily medication for a while, and it's important to start with light but regular exercise. Certain aspects of your relationship with your husband may inevitably change as well. However, both of you will adjust to all of this over time.

"And you need to continue the fight for survival. The next step is to start you on chemotherapy, but you will receive it as an outpatient.

"Just be prepared, chemotherapy will weaken your system and can compromise the immune system. I have arranged a meeting with an oncologist, to explain the process to you so that you know what to expect."

We were scheduled to meet the oncologist the following day. Dr. Blanden, the head oncologist, took the time to explain chemotherapy to us, providing thorough information on both the potential side effects and the benefits of the treatment.

"Chemotherapy helps to slow the growth of secondary tumours in the chest and prevents it from spreading to new areas.

"We will administer your chemotherapy intravenously (into a vein), using a drug called cytotoxic. The course of treatment will be broken into eight cycles, each cycle lasting about three weeks. You will have a week's rest after each cycle.

"The complete course will take six months. You might suffer some side effects like hair loss, tiredness, vomiting, muscle and joint aches, or diarrhoea," he explained.

The explanation was over, and Comfort's medication was prepared for her. We then awaited the discharge letter, which contained crucial information for her GP. Shortly after, it was handed to her.

It was hard to say goodbye to the amazing hospital staff, but on the other hand, we were also delighted that Comfort had survived the ordeal and was ready to return to the family.

We said our goodbyes to everyone and departed for home. Upon getting to the house, she hugged both boys and expressed how much she had missed them. Then she went to bed and slept for a full eight hours, like a newborn.

On the first day of Comfort's chemotherapy treatment, following our meeting with Dr. Blanden, we were taken on a visit to the chemo infusion suite where the toxic infusions were administered. Inside the suite, we observed other patients accompanied by their families and friends, all undergoing treatment. I was also present with my wife to provide support during this challenging time.

Mary, the nurse, introduced herself and explained the procedure to us, "First, we will need to insert a port, a thin piece of metal, into the skin of the chest to inject the chemicals directly into it. Each session will last about five hours, which we will closely monitor."

"I am so worried, terrified about the whole idea of chemotherapy," Comfort said. "I have heard that chemotherapy does not distinguish between the healthy and bad cells, but kills everything," she lamented.

The nurse quickly gave her some assurance, "Many people have gone through the process with us, and it wasn't as bad as you might imagine. They all coped well after the treatment. They were a bit tired, but after some time they were all fine and well again." the nurse assured Comfort.

"My first day at the chemo infusion suite, the nurse prepared me for the first treatment. She stuck a big needle through the little piece of metal that had been put into my chest skin and administered the chemicals," Comfort explained after coming back to meet me in the recovery ward.

After her treatment Comfort felt weak, frail, dizzy, nauseous, and exhausted. She vomited, felt like her head was spinning, and was moaning in pain. After she recovered, I took her home by taxi.

Comfort is now in the final days of her chemotherapy treatment. She has undergone months of chemotherapy facing numerous challenges along the way such as going bald and looking so frail.

"My cancer has finally disappeared, after three years," Comfort said with relief.

After three years, the nurse was happy to remove Comfort's port. We were overjoyed that we would soon have this horror behind us.

On the day the port was removed, the area was first numbed with local anaesthetic. The doctor made a small incision, lifted the piece of metal, and gently pulled it out of her chest.

After the minor surgery, we left for home feeling excited, reflecting on the entire journey.

A year after her cancer treatment, we were finally ready to return to Nigeria – back to our roots. It was time to go home for good.

The house was put on the market again and this time we were fortunate. It sold quickly. After deducting the necessary agent's fee and the remaining mortgage owed, the profit was more than enough for us to move back to Nigeria.

CHAPTER 17

The Return to Nigeria

I had arranged to meet Joan and Mary in a restaurant near her house to inform them that I am finally preparing to leave for Nigeria. This would give me the opportunity to meet my daughter Joan for the last time before moving back to Nigeria.

On the day of our meeting, I had arranged we meet at the MacDonalds restaurant very near her house. I was so delighted to see Joan, my daughter, and we had lots of discussions. I explained to her that her dad will be returning to my homeland, but I promised to stay in touch with her. I also assured her that when she is older, I would send her an invitation to come visit me in Nigeria.

The feeling of leaving her was overwhelming. It was a night filled with mixed emotions. I kissed my daughter on the cheek and whispered, "I will be back soon." After dinner, we all went our separate ways.

We bought our flight tickets and bid farewell to all our friends in London. The most difficult part was saying goodbye to Father Morgan. I called him to inform him that we would visit him to say our farewells as we had perfected our travel plans.

Father Morgan, my inspirational mentor, was delighted for me. He was happy that I had achieved my goal of becoming a lawyer and was now ready to use the knowledge I gained in my native country.

On the appointed day, I brought Comfort and the boys to see him one last time. We spent the entire afternoon and evening with him, soaking in his wise words and receiving valuable advice. Before we left, Father Morgan prayed with us, and we exchanged heartfelt hugs. I promised to stay in touch with him once we were settled back in Nigeria.

On the day of our flight, some friends accompanied us to the Heathrow airport.

I had already sent a telegram to my father, informing him of my arrival date and time. The anticipation of finally returning home filled me with excitement.

I embraced each of my friends who came to see me off at the airport, waved goodbye and proceeded through the departure lounge, and that was it. With mixed emotions, we boarded the airplane and soon soared high above the London sky, beginning our journey back to Nigeria.

After nearly twelve hours in the air, our plane eventually touched down at Lagos airport. We disembarked and proceeded through the immigration and custom checks. Walking towards the arrivals area, I couldn't help but reflect on my journey. *I went to London alone, and here I am returning home with my wife and two children, armed with my hard-earned certificate as a qualified lawyer*. I was enjoying every bit of my arrival.

As we strolled through the arrival lounge, my father was quick to spot me. I glanced at him, feeling overwhelmed with joy at seeing him again after all these years—12 years that seemed to have passed in the blink of an eye. He looked much older than when I had left him and Mum.

It dawned on me then that time inevitably catches up with those we hold dear. Dad had wrinkled, and Mum's hair had turned grey.

Standing beside them were Comfort's parents. I greeted all of them, prostrating as our custom demands. Dad attempted to lift me up, but his strength failed him, so he held me upright to prevent me from bending down completely. He understood that I was now a grown man. I clung to him tightly, overcome with emotion. Tears welled up in my eyes as I grappled with the reality of seeing these once vibrant individuals now displaying signs of aging.

"No need to cry, Biyi. Today is meant to be a joyous day. Don't cry. Be a man, as you have always been," Dad comforted me, handing me his handkerchief to wipe my tears.

Comfort also followed tradition, kneeling as she greeted everyone respectfully.

Before we left London, I had explained to the children that they will also have to prostrate to greet all the elderly people. I introduced them to my parents and Comfort's parents. They were happy to see both of them. The children prostrated to greet them as our custom demands without disappointing us.

Everyone was so thrilled to see us again. They were also delighted to finally see their grandchildren after such a long time.

Dad had also brought some town elders to Lagos, and I greeted them with respect.

We made our way to the parking area, where they had hired a large bus to transport us all. To our surprise and delight, as we neared the bus, drums were beating, creating a festive atmosphere.

Those inside the bus were in costume and masks, singing and dancing joyously to welcome my family and celebrate our return.

We left the airport and headed for our town.

As we reached the border between my hometown and the neighbouring town, Ilishan Remo, we were greeted by an entourage of elders, masquerades and locals also dressed in colourful attire and masks.

The entire town was in a festive mood, eagerly awaiting the arrival of their beloved son.

I stepped out of the bus to join the procession, feeling overwhelmed by the warmth of the welcome.

The masqueraders were dancing, singing traditional songs, accompanied by drums. Comfort and the children and I danced with wild abandon. I felt like I had not danced forever.

It was such a moment of joy in my life, to return to my people, to my much beloved Irolu Remo.

Upon arriving at the family house, my dad's house, a customary ritual awaited me before I could enter. Libations of palm wine were poured, accompanied by prayers offered to express gratitude for my safe return to my hometown. Additionally, a ram was swiftly sacrificed as a symbolic gesture to appease the gods and ensure continued blessings and protection for my family and me.

To my surprise dad had extended the house, adding three-bedroom flat in anticipation of my return. He ushered me in with my family and told me, "These is your flat, for you and your family."

With deep gratitude, I prostrated before him to express my immense appreciation for this thoughtful gesture.

Then there was a lot to eat and drink, including the traditional palm wine, which I had missed so much. Mum and her family and my in-laws had prepared lots of food for all the visitors. My happiness was immeasurable. My dad and mum kept gazing at me with a mixture of disbelief and joy, as if I was a visitor from another planet; they could not quite believe I was back with them in Irolu Remo.

They still could not believe that I was finally back home, after twelve years. In some ways, it felt like it was just like yesterday.

They were also happy at being able to witness this joyous occasion while they were still alive, especially with the added joy of meeting their other grandsons.

To add to the nostalgic atmosphere, my mother had lovingly prepared my favourite meal: pounded yam with bush meat and vegetables, just like the good old days.

I had long thought about it, yearning for it badly. It seemed as though my mother could read my thoughts. I did miss this!

I was filled with indescribable joy to be home again, among my people, my kinsmen. We shared food, drink, and lively conversation, unable to contain our excitement. My parents and Comfort's parents couldn't take their eyes off their new grandson, as if still processing the reality of his presence. I was now given the opportunity to thank and address all the people present at the gathering.

"I thank God and the spirit of our ancestors for guiding me safely back home and helping me to achieve the Golden Fleece.

"I thank my wife, Comfort, who stood by me, and to my children for their love and understanding. I extend my gratitude to my parents, my in-laws, and all the esteemed town elders of Irolu Remo. Returning to my roots and being surrounded by my people fills me with immense joy. I am especially thankful that all of you are here to welcome me back. This moment is truly priceless, and I cannot express how grateful I am."

"The journey for my success was long and challenging. I never thought it would take so long but our forefathers never abandoned me. My time in the white man's land exposed me to remarkable experiences and taught me new ways of doing things. I am confident that the knowledge I have gained will be valuable first to my people in Irolu Remo and here in Nigeria.

"And finally, thank you all for coming here today to celebrate with us. Your presence has made this occasion truly special," I said.

Everybody was amused at my story. They were all delighted for me. I was proud of myself. They were amused that I still spoke my Remo dialect perfectly to the astonishment of my children. They have never seen me speaking in Remo dialect.

I immediately showed my Golden Fleece to them all. My parents were so happy when I showed them my certificate as a qualified lawyer with work experience in the United Kingdom. I handed it to my father and later to my mum and all the elders to have a look. Though most of them could not read what was inside.

"Is that the way the Certificate looks like", one of the elders asked. Yes, I said to him.

The town's chief priest then stepped forward and said, "I thank everyone present today. Our forefathers never abandoned our children. We are happy for the safe arrival of our son and his family from the white man's land. May God and the spirit of our ancestors continue to guide you in all your endeavours."

"Amen," echoed everyone present.

The celebration continued until daybreak, with the children retiring to bed early due to exhaustion from the journey. Eventually, fatigue caught up with me too. Glancing at Comfort, I noticed she was beginning to drift off as well. Yawning as a form of been exhausted and tired

We all had a deep, long, refreshing sleep, and then gradually settled back into our hometown.

I remained in my town for about two weeks after our arrival from London. Many visitors came to welcome me and my family back to town.

Now a celebrity, everyone clamoured to catch a glimpse of me - a traditional worshipper transformed into a lawyer with Western educated man.

To many of the younger generation, I became an inspirational figure.

My parents beamed with pride at my achievements.

Comfort and the other women diligently prepared special meals each day, while people indulged in drinks regularly.

Visitors often began arriving at our house as early as 7:00 am. While I appreciated their eagerness to see me, it sometimes proved inconvenient, requiring me to wake up early to attend to them with a smile on my face.

Early in the morning, Dad headed to his farm, as was his routine. He rose at dawn to collect fresh palm wine and hunt bush rats for our dinner. Mum promptly grilled the bush rat in hot chilli pepper.

We all sat under the shade tree by our house, enjoying palm wine and the grilled bush rat, relishing every bite.

Dad filled me in on the town's developments during my absence.

"We have a new king now. Kabiyesi Sofunke passed away," he informed me.

"I believe he was not as old as his predecessor," I said.

"No, you are correct. He wasn't. But he suffered a stroke and was bedridden for a year before passing away peacefully," Dad responded.

"He received a full traditional burial, according to our customs. Ten cows along with goats, sheep, chickens, and turkeys, were slaughtered to appease the gods. The entire town mourned for over six months.

"Women were confined to their homes for an entire week, and sacrifices were made to the deity Oro for six months to purify the town, allowing his spirit to join his ancestors.

"As you know, our town is governed by seven ruling houses. It was the turn of our house, 'Osanpon Erikose,' to nominate the next king. However, the selection process became highly contested between two families: your two uncles – Abdul and Adewole. Both were eager to ascend to the throne.

"The family convened a meeting of elders to settle the matter, but it remained unresolved, leading them to resort to legal intervention. Uncle Abdul, with the assistance of his lawyer, attempted to bribe the judge, coming dangerously close to success until his actions were exposed to the public."

"Both the judge and Uncle Abdul received death threats prompting them to relocate from the town. Uncle Adewole was declared the winner and was crowned the king.

"A new secondary school was also built through communal effort, eliminating the need for children to trek two miles daily to the nearest school. Now, five years later, the first set of students has graduated. Some have even secured employment as teachers to support the new primary school.

"Furthermore, a new police station and a dispensary have been established. Previously, the town grappled with a scarcity of potable water. Thanks to rain harvesting, which fills the Isa (mud tanks), we now have sufficient water for year-round consumption.

"The government constructed a new water station along the River Uren in Ikenne, the neighboring town, to supply water to our town consistently throughout the year.

Furthermore, our town is now linked to the national grid, providing us with uninterrupted electricity! This achievement owes much to the efforts of the late Kabiyesi's son, Olanrewaju, who worked with the Nigerian Electricity Corporation and facilitated this.

"It cost two thousand, eight hundred pounds. Access to electricity has helped our town to do more poultry farming and set up plants for cassava production and pounded yam processing.

"Also, our roads are now tarred and much smoother to drive on, and we have our own local radio station in the town, voice of Irolu Remo.

"Our town has become part of a new local government council,(Ikenne Local government council) comprising the towns of Ikenne, Ilishan, Irolu, Iperu, and Ogere.

"There are new political groups emerging around the country, and our region is now governed by the 'Action Group Party.' Our counsellor happens to be one of your younger cousins from your mother's family," father explained.

This conversation with my father lasted the entire day, as he moved from one topic to another.

As it was December when I returned to Nigeria with my family, this would be my first celebration of Christmas and the New Year in my hometown in over twelve years.

I was looking forward to the town festivities during this month, when many of our native friends would journey home from Lagos, Ibadan, and the surrounding areas to reunite with their loved ones.

It would indeed be a joyous occasion for the whole family to be together after such a long time. Most of my friends who learnt I was finally back in our village came to visit me, their faces beaming with delight. It was heartwarming to see them again. Most had matured, with some even sporting grey hairs. Their presence filled me with happiness after such a long absence.

CHAPTER 18

The Death of My African Woman

After two weeks of Christmas and New Year celebrations, I travelled to Lagos with my children and Comfort to stay with my mother's immediate brother, Uncle Biodun. He serves as a director at one of the ministries in Lagos. We had previously met in the village when I arrived from London during visits to our family.

Fortunately, during our time in the village, I informed him of my plans to come to Lagos for my registration with the Nigerian Law School in Victoria Island, which is conveniently close to where he resides.

He graciously agreed to accommodate my family during our stay. This arrangement would also allow me the opportunity to find permanent accommodation and familiarise myself with Lagos and its surroundings.

Even though I had completed my law education in the United Kingdom, I needed to attend Nigerian law school for a year to obtain the necessary certification to practice here in Nigeria.

After extensive searching without luck, Uncle Biodun introduced me to one of his colleagues, an estate agent, who found an impressive property for sale. We decided to look at it, and upon our initial inspection, we were immediately impressed. The property was a newly built one-storey building adorned with sleek brown brick exteriors. It consisted of four spacious flats, each boasting modern amenities. Additionally, it had its water supply system featuring a borehole with four tanks situated on the flat roof. The property also included a small parking lot with enough space for four cars. It was truly an impressive find.

Each flat had three bedrooms, all with en suite bathrooms, as well as a kitchen, dining room, and living room. Every unit came fully furnished, providing convenience for the occupants. Surrounding the building were expansive flower beds adorned with vibrant native flowers, adding to the aesthetic appeal. The complex was equipped with an entry gate and a security guard for added safety. Additionally, there was a garden area where we could cultivate vegetables and fruits. We opted for the first floor flat situated at the front of the building, offering a view of the main road and overlooking a serene landscape of trees. The cherry on top was its proximity to where I was starting my course.

From the moment Comfort, the children, and I laid eyes on the building and the flat, we fell in love with it. It was perfect! We completed the necessary documentation and made the payment promptly. Anxious to settle into our new home, we wasted no time transferring our belongings from my father's house in the village where we had been staying. We only made a few minor adjustments to the flat before settling in.

I registered at the Nigerian Law School to fulfil the requirement for practicing law in Nigeria. The initial three months were dedicated to qualifying for Bar 1, where we were introduced to the Nigerian legal system and the subsequent nine months, known as Bar 2, focused on equipping foreign-trained lawyers with the knowledge and skills necessary to practice Nigerian law. During this period, I devoted time to observing court proceedings and familiarizing myself with the Nigerian legal system by spending time in courtrooms and legal offices.

After completing the one-year program, I successfully passed the Board of Benches examination, and my certificate was ratified by the Supreme Court, officially granting me the title of Nigerian barrister. Subsequently, I pursued specialization in constitutional law and secured a position at Albert Chambers, a prestigious legal firm well known in Lagos. Meanwhile, Comfort used her education in the United Kingdom to her advantage and secured a job as a nurse at the Lagos General Hospital in Marina, Lagos. Her qualifications positioned her as the top candidate among many applicants. She was offered the position of matron at the hospital because of her vast experience in nursing, having worked at the Royal London hospital Whitechapel in the United Kingdom.

Success seemed to be a thread running through our family, with each member achieving milestones. My sons, now aged twenty-five and eleven, were making significant strides. My eldest son was nearing the completion of his studies at Lagos University, where he was pursuing a degree in Economics and Business Management. Meanwhile, my younger son was on the verge of starting his secondary school education.

As an aspiring politician, I aligned myself with the Action Group political party and was nominated to be the local parliamentary candidate for my constituency. The community rallied behind my campaign, recognizing my expertise as a constitutional lawyer.

The election was fiercely competitive between my party (the Action group) and the National Party of Nigeria. After a long night of vote counting, the results were finally announced, and I emerged victorious. I was officially declared the winner and duly elected to represent my Remo North constituency.

The joy of victory was palpable among my family, Comfort, and the children. We celebrated my parliamentary success with overwhelming happiness and gratitude. As preparations began for my swearing-in ceremony, Comfort suddenly fell ill. She complained of a severe headache, lamenting that her whole head was pounding. Sleep eluded her the entire night.

At one point, in the middle of the night, she woke me up. "Biyi, the headache is so severe and unbearable, I can't sleep," she said, clutching her head in pain. I said, "Just relax and put your head on my chest." She did and fell asleep immediately, looking more beautiful than ever.

The next morning, I left Comfort to rest in bed and went to take a shower. I returned to the room and found her awake, and she asked about breakfast. As she got up and headed towards the door, she suddenly stopped, clutched her head, and mumbled, "Biyi, hea…" before collapsing.

This happened suddenly, and it brought me into panic mode as I heard a big bang; she had lost her grip on the door and was on the floor.

Comfort, Comfort, Comfort I screamed. Thinking of the worst, I saw her head crash into the door, as she tried hard to hold onto the door handle. I screamed again, "Comfort! Comfort! Comfort!" I called out to the boys, who were also petrified to see their mum on the floor after hearing a big bang.

The three of us panicked but gathered courage. With the boys' assistance, bewildered and still in shock to see their mother in such a terrible condition, we carried her to the car. At that moment, I felt the same waves of fear that had gripped me when a similar incident occurred back in England.

As I was driving, it became harder to see. My vision became blurred.

I could not comprehend why the front windshield of the car was wet until my elder son said, "Dad, stop crying, and please be strong for Mum."

We soon arrived at the nearest hospital, and Comfort was wheeled into the hospital. She was admitted straight away.

They carried out various tests, including a CAT scan. While waiting for the result, I found myself feeling like I did in London when I first received the devastating news of Comfort's cancer diagnosis. The familiar feelings of dread and helplessness washed over me once again, intensifying the gravity of the situation.

When the results finally arrived. The head consultant asked me to come in, and he wanted to speak with me. I lost it and started shouting, "what is it? What is the situation? He asked me to calm down. I was panting and waiting for the news.

It was the inevitable news we had feared.

The Consultant informed me that the cancer had returned, and her condition was now terminal. Despite undergoing chemotherapy, the cancer had spread rapidly to multiple organs, rendering her helpless. The doctors and nurses solemnly prepared us for the worst.

"Oh my God!" I screamed, water gushing out of my eyes. I found it difficult to explain to our boys their mum's terminal condition. I just summoned the courage to tell them she was ill and all would be fine by God's grace. But by my tears, they suspected all was not well.

Every day after work, I visited her, and we would have a lot of discussions about our life journey, our relationship, and our boys.

Comfort was now frail...

I took an extended leave from work to be by her side in the hospital. Each day, I left home in the morning and returned late in the evening. Three weeks sped by, and there was still no improvement. Comfort endured excruciating pain throughout her body, crying out in agony each day. It was traumatic to witness her suffering daily like this.

After one month and a day while with Comfort in the hospital, she uttered those haunting words: "My death is now a reality. I will soon be gone. It will happen. Take good care of the children." Her words pierced through my heart, leaving me feeling utterly helpless and devastated. All I could do was sit beside her on the hospital bed and clasp her hands tightly in mine. Our sons were nearby, their distress palpable. We devoted every moment we could to be with her during her final days, praying fervently as a family for a miracle to happen.

In those sacred hours, we clung to each other, holding our hands tightly together and praying. Comfort was dying, struggling to breathe, and taking deep, heavy breaths.

"Ayodele, Ayodele, go and call the nurse urgently," I instructed one of the boys. He dashed off immediately.

However, in the brief moments that followed, Comfort took her final breath; she breathed very deep and heavy. My heart shattered as I wept bitterly, gently closing her eyes with my hand. By the time the children returned with the nurses, Comfort had passed away. She had departed to join our ancestors. The children's cries of "Mum! Mum! Mum! filled the room, but there was no response from Comfort.

They held her hands, but there was no movement. Their anguish erupted into deep sobs as they realized she was not responding and no longer with us. I held them close, offering whatever comfort I could as we navigated the overwhelming grief together.

Comfort, my African girl, my first love, my wife, the mother of my children, my confidante, and my African woman, died peacefully in my arms.

I love you and will forever love you. Till we meet again, to part no more. May your gentle soul continue to rest in perfect peace with the Almighty. Amen.

"Comfort as you embark on a journey of no return, may the spirits of our ancestors be with you Ase" meaning amen. Those are my last words as I bid her farewell.

Good night, my angel.

ABOUT AUTHOR

Dr. Adeleke Oyenusi was born on November 12, 1961, in Irolu Remo, Ogun State, Nigeria. He hails from a royal lineage, the grandson of the late King Oba Joseph Sofunke Oyenusi, who reigned over Irolu Remo from 1926 to 1964.

His educational journey commenced at Methodist Primary School, Ekotedo, Ibadan, Oyo State, in 1967. Following his father's transfer to Lagos, he continued his studies at Holy Trinity School in Ebute Ero, Lagos, from 1970 to 1973. Subsequently, he pursued his secondary education at Methodist Secondary Commercial College, Sagamu, Ogun State, from 1973 to 1977.

After excelling in his WAEC examinations, he briefly served as a primary school teacher in Ipara Remo, Ogun State, Nigeria. Later, he pursued advanced-level studies at Remo Secondary School in Sagamu Remo, Ogun State, from 1978 to 1980. His academic prowess earned him a government scholarship to study in the former USSR in 1981.

Dr. Oyenusi embarked on his educational journey in Kharkiv, Ukraine, where he undertook a Russian language course from 1981 to 1982. Subsequently, he continued his studies in Minsk, Belarus, graduating with a first-class Master's Degree in National Economic Planning in 1987. He then pursued further studies in Moscow, Russian Republic, where he obtained his doctorate in economics in 1992.

In 1996, Dr. Oyenusi relocated to London, where he underwent teacher's training. During this period, he worked at Trans-Atlantic College and Westminster College London. Despite encountering health challenges, he persevered, and today, we are thankful for his resilience and strength.

Dr. Oyenusi is a proud father of three children: Princess Kimberlyne, Kelvin, and Kenneth Oyenusi. Additionally, he has authored two books titled "Living a Normal and Healthy Life after Renal (Kidney) Failure Part 1" and "My Kidney Transplantation Part 2." His linguistic abilities extend beyond English to Russian, French, Yoruba, Lingala, and Ijebu.

Milton Keynes UK
Ingram Content Group UK Ltd.
UKHW050417030824
446490UK00008B/308